A Travel in Time to Grand Pré

Michele Doucette

A Travel in Time to Grand Pré

ISBN 978-0-9801704-6-7

Printed in the United States of America by

St. Clair Publications

PO Box 726

McMinnville, TN   37111-0726

stclairpublications.com

The quality of our world depends upon the quality of our thoughts as individuals. If the majority of individuals are positive and successful, then society itself will naturally be positive, successful and prosperous; however, if the majority of people are negative, hateful and unsuccessful, then people will live in unhappy, unsuccessful, and perhaps even dire circumstances. In keeping with *As A Man Thinketh* by James Allen, so, too, thinketh a society. It is simple cause and effect. When you look at it this way, it is as if we each have a responsibility to be positive and to help others be positive. If you will take it upon yourself to condition your mind to be positive, to help other people, to be successful, to fill your life with happiness, then I have accomplished one of my primary objectives; for you see, if you help two people, and they help two people, it is through the miraculous power of compound growth that we can create massive social improvement for us all that will spread throughout the world.

William H. Marshall, author of *Power Affirmations: Power Positive Conditioning For Your Subconscious Mind*

Table of Contents

Reviews

Having read *A Travel in Time to Grand Pré* by Michele Doucette, I am amazed at her ability to combine time travel with the proclaimed holy bloodline and Acadian history. In this story, the reader feels the sensation of traveling back to the eighteenth century, and seeing history in the making. Likewise, it is a story of enduring love. She keeps the reader's attention, leaving the door open for a sequel.

Michele's transition from a research writer to a novelist is truly remarkable. Anyone with an interest in these themes should delve into this fascinating drama. Well researched, well presented and well documented, I congratulate Michele on a gripping novel.

Stanley J. St. Clair, author of <u>Prayers of Prophets, Knights and Kings and Mysterious People of the Bible In the Light of History</u>

A Travel in Time to Grand Pré

A Travel in Time to Grand Pré is a historically informative adventure, tying the history of the descendants of Yeshua (also known as Jesus) to modern day Nova Scotia, Canada.

Madeleine Sinclair feels disconnected with the era of her birth, yet intuitively aware of herself in another time period in history. Transported back to 1754 Acadie, she comes to learn, live and experience firsthand the lives of the French Acadian people, meeting Michel *dit Sophie* LeBlanc, her love of that time.

Through the warm, loving and helpful guidance of fellow time traveler, Madame Pêche, she comes to understand the predetermined course of her Sinclair bloodline, beginning with Rollo the Viking, father of William Longsword, a line that is shown to be linked to the Merovingians, the Cathars and the Knights Templar (protectors of the Holy Grail).

Before long, the reader is led to the very apex of this time travel adventure for Madeleine has been decreed *the one* who is to introduce the words of Yeshua, spoken in Aramaic at the height of his ministry, to the modern world.

Herein, Yeshua explains how individuals can find their way, their truth(s), so as to live their lives to the fullest.

Introducing some new historical perspectives, debut novelist Michele Doucette delivers a compelling, fascinating read that is sure to please.

Suzanne Olsson, author of <u>Jesus in Kashmir: The Lost Tomb</u> <u>and co-author of Roza Bal: The Tomb of Jesus</u>

Michele Doucette has created a wonderful and beautiful piece in *A Travel in Time to Grand Pré*. Interesting and well developed, this story grabs the reader and takes them on a most entertaining journey. In keeping with her talent, she is able to weave powerful metaphysical messages that can only assist each reader in striving to reach a more profound, and individualized, spiritual understanding of life.

I strongly suggest that you grab a copy and sit down where you shant be disturbed.

Elio Serra, USA

Entertaining, fun, educational and visionary, an exciting and grand book, I read it all in one fell swoop. With an excellent ability to sift through ideas and blend concepts, it is so well done that she creates a vision we can all easily align with. Kudos to Michele and her outstanding writing skills in knitting together this beautiful story of time travel, love, remembrance and adventure; clearly, such an extraordinary depiction can only be recommended as a book for readers of all ages.

Joelle Houze, D. Ac., D.D., author of <u>Touching the Life Force</u> and <u>Dancing With God</u>

Captivated from the start, I felt as if I was Madeleine; so much so, in fact, that I just *had* to keep reading. Michele Doucette has found the means to make the learning of the history of a people both fun and entertaining, which is a special gift. I am looking forward to the sequel.

Christina Hawco, Canada

A Travel in Time to Grand Pré is a wonderful journey on the esoteric road, one which serves to unveil part of the stories as to why the Acadians, and the latter Creoles, Cajuns and Métis, experienced such upheavals.

The main Norman and Templar families interwoven with the origin of Acadia and earlier settlements in the new world will tantalize and inspire readers of all genres.

Martin Carriere, Canada

Michele's passion for genealogy, history, mysticism and metaphysics comes through loudly in *A Travel in Time to Grand Pr*é. Her writing style makes for an easy read and propels you from one page to the next. She writes from the heart and thus makes her characters come alive. There is a wealth of information hidden in this novel and the reader is being educated without even being aware of it. Very well written, I heartily recommend this book.

Linda Earle, Canada

I finished *A Travel in Time to Grand Pré* in one sitting. This book was awesome. I do not know how Michele does it, seamlessly weaving such a great (and to me, believable) story of time travel into all of the tons of research that it took to put this thoughtful and emotionally compelling story together. I am truly amazed. Keep up the great writing. I am anxious to find out what happens next.

Genn Waite, USA

A Travel in Time to Grand Pré is a spectacular journey to infinity. Never before have I read such a book. The genius of Michele Doucette's writing shows in a grand manner, yet the reader never sees her ego lurking on those precious pages where the storyline follows times long past, recreating moments of excitement and love.

This touching story, a well researched moment in history, is written in an almost mystical style which I have not encountered before. *A Travel in Time to Grand Pré* is an Acadian novel with a French touch, but even the French do not write with Michele's elegance; sparse and yet effective.

To me, this book is magical and visionary; the more often I read it, the deeper in time I find myself. There is always something new, and it feels like Michele has hidden it there for the reader to find.

Raita Outinen, Journalist, Finland

A Travel in Time to Grand Pré is a most fascinating read. Michele successfully draws the reader into a deep spiritual adventure exploring concepts of time travel and quantum physics as well as the mysteries of the Holy Grail.

I have personally studied these same subjects of the Cathars, Knights Templar and Merovingians, as well as the theories of the Holy Grail, and yet I was totally amazed at how expertly Michele wove this story together with Acadian, Mi'kmaq and Scottish history, bringing it all into modern relevance.

This story was exciting, gripping and most unexpected. Above all, the spiritual message throughout gives each reader much to take away as nourishment for the soul.

A wonderful book I can wholeheartedly recommend to enthrall.

Elizabeth Hamilton, Australia

A Travel in Time to Grand Pré is a fascinating read by author Michele Doucette. The reader will be captivated by her cleverness to create this beautiful story of love and Acadian history, interwoven with spiritual messages to further enhance the delectable journey of time travel.

With an ability to weave a dynamic storyline that is clearly apparent in this book, I am looking forward to reading the sequel.

Bettye Johnson, author of <u>The Secrets of the Magdalene Scrolls</u> and <u>Mary Magdalene, Her Story</u>

Beautifully written, I very much appreciate how Michele has incorporated the Mi'kmaq history into that of the Sinclair line while tying them both together to the early Norman families, as well as to the Cathars, to the Merovingians, to Yeshua, and even further back to the Pharaohs of Egypt. Michele has a flare for captivating the audience by enabling the reader to experience moments of history through pivotal events and occurrences in time, whilst adding some creative imagination. I found it incredibly emotional to read what the Acadians had to endure during the deportation.

Michele takes it even further by adding our most primal senses of being from our maker, reminding us of some great morals that we sometimes forget to live by in this demanding and fast paced world. She awakens us to remembering that change is at hand, for it is through our own actions that we can make an appreciable difference.

An absolutely fabulous read for all.

Diana Sinclair, Canada

A Travel in Time to Grand Pré

From the striking bronze Grand Pré sculpture featured on the inside cover, to the first few pages and then the entire book, this most innovative and imaginative tale held my attention from the get go. Michele Doucette weaves a fascinating story about Madeleine Sinclair, a young time traveler, inspired by Henry Wadsworth Longfellow's <u>Evangeline</u>, who travels back in time to fulfill her destiny, meeting some interesting people in the process. She also provides a taste of Acadian life, an aperitif of things to come, which, while romantic, also provides a glimpse to the realities of settler life in the colonies.

Included in this spiritual and historical adventure is an indigenous Mi'kmaq, young Gabriel Sinclair, descended from Henry Sinclair, an early pre-Columbian American explorer. He passes on to her a priceless Templar taonga, an Aramaic treasure, gifted to the world by Yeshua, which returns with her to the twenty-first century. This is a truly gripping, nostalgic and poignant Holy Grail story, expertly woven and full of intrigue; not to be missed, this is one publication to be read and savored.

Jim Sinclair, New Zealand

A Travel in Time to Grand Pré captured my imagination and interest immediately. Michele Doucette's unique style and blend of such disciplines as Acadian history, genealogy and spirituality with fiction, kept me tuning page after page. I lost track of time as I traveled with Madeleine to the mid 1700's. Living the story, I both experienced the love, wonder and excitement of her discoveries, as well as debilitating pain and utter anguish at the deportation of the Acadian people.

This historical novel has all the makings of a delightfully depicted blockbuster of a movie!

Bride Doyle, author of *Quest for Happiness: Handling Difficult Relationships Using The FTA Approach*

A Travel in Time to Grand Pré is a beautifully written tale of a young woman's spiritual journey through time. When Madeleine Sinclair suddenly finds herself catapulted back in time, she begins an astonishing journey of discovery. Who is she, really? What secrets are hidden in her DNA?

Author Michele Doucette manages to weave a tapestry rich with culture, history, romance and humanity. This wonderful adventure will leave the reader thinking about the endless mysteries and possibilities that each of us carry within us on this journey we call life.

Claudette (Ravenmoonstar) Kennedy, USA

Deportation sculpture in Grand Pré, Nova Scotia, marks the centre of the Acadian settlement from 1682 to 1755. Image ID 43286590 @ Meunierd | Dreamstime.com

Author's Note

I wish to thank both Kevin Kendall (initial designer) and Kent Hesselbein (current designer) for the stunningly beautiful cover design. In truth, both of these gentlemen were instrumental in being able to capture the essence of my feelings in the creation of a vision far more hauntingly beautiful than I was anticipating.

As my husband is so fond of saying ... *within reach is what is attainable; beyond reach is what is imaginable.*

May you, too, reach for the imaginable by listening to your heart and remaining true to what you already know.

With over 6.5 billion people sharing this planet, this means that there are 6.5 billion realities, viewpoints, truths, opinions and ways of expressing.

You simply have to recognize that which is yours, for you, alone, must walk your path.

Dedication

It has been a life-long dream of mine to publish a book in paperback format. It is with great delight that I formally dedicate this work to many individuals of great importance.

The women who instilled in me a strong love for my Acadian ancestry: my maternal grandmother, Catherine (Kay) Breau, and great grandmother, Marie Philomène Mallet; herein lie my connections to both northern New Brunswick and Québec.

I would also like to think that my ability to arrange the written word with efficacy has been freely inherited through my maternal grandfather, James Henry (Harry) Feeley.

Acting as his personal secretary, I can say with absolute conviction that he was the best of storytellers. With a wee bit of Irish thrown into the gene pool for good measure, it may very well be as a result of this leprechaun believer that I have been able to weave my own brand of magic.

Although I did not know my paternal Acadian grandparents, Jean Avite (Harvey) Doucette and Beatrice Muise, both grandpère and grandmère have never been far from my thoughts; herein lie my connections to the Yarmouth area of Nova Scotia.

I was blessed to have known Lesley Anne Doucet, a dear Acadian cousin, from Yarmouth, albeit for too short a time. Continuing to remain brave in her battle with Neimann-Pick Disease, she transitioned on January 15, 2003, at the tender age of eighteen years.

As always, my husband, Albert. After twenty-four years of dedication to each other, he remains my own special hero.

Acknowledgments

What makes a good writer? Someone who writes what they know, someone who writes from the heart, someone who writes with passion. I do my utmost to adhere to all three noteworthy components.

Throughout the writing of this book, I was continuously encouraged by my husband's unwavering belief in my ability to pen words to paper.

I trust that my children, Alyssa and Niall, will be proud of this written effort that their mother has made. In addition, I know that they, too, will locate their artistic passions so as to enjoy their own adventures in this game we call life.

There are many other people to whom I owe special thanks, namely:

[1] Roger Pierre Aubé, a dear Acadian cousin who took me through northern New Brunswick in 1998 whereby we spent Acadian Day (August 15) in Caraquet.

On the final leg of the journey, we also took the time to visit the National Historic Park in Grand Pré, donning our costumes of Gabriel and Evangeline.

[2] Kenneth Breau, maternal cousin, and archivist at the Université de Moncton, whom I was privileged to meet while touring in 1998.

[3] David MacLeod, a Maine cousin who was the first to share with me the air of mystery surrounding Doucet brothers, Pierre (1621) and Germain (1641).

[4] Paul Pierre Bourgeois, of Grand-Digue, New Brunswick, author of À la recherche des Bourgeois d'Acadie (1614 à 1800), cousin and email correspondent of many years who, sadly, passed away in November 2007.

[5] Léo Doucet, a dear Acadian cousin who did his best to coach me through many of my Family Tree Maker gedcom glitches before my Family Origins defection.

[6] Lucie LeBlanc Consentino, cousin and webmistress of Acadian and French Canadian Ancestral Home, who continues to provide me with significant genealogical assistance.

[7] Pauline d'Entremont, a dear Acadian cousin who always attempts to find an answer to my seemingly endless barrage of questions pertaining to my roots in Yarmouth County, Nova Scotia.

[8] Claudette (Ravenmoonstar) Kennedy, for taking the time to read my manuscript whilst also offering contributions, courtesy of our metaphysical email conversations.

[9] Stanley J. St. Clair, author of <u>Mysterious People of the Bible In the Light of History</u>, for taking the time to read my manuscript, offering countless publication tips.

[10] Suzanne (Indiana Sue) Olsson, author of <u>Jesus in Kashmir: The Lost Tomb</u> and co-author of <u>Roza Bal: The Tomb of Jesus</u>, for taking the time to read my manuscript, offering countless words of wisdom.

[11] Linda Earle, a local soul sister; always there for me, she demonstrates the strength of the female Celtic warrior, Boudicca, a name meaning *victorious*.

[12] Betty Dobson, owner/operator of InkSpotter Publishing in Halifax, Nova Scotia. As my editor, she helped me turn a fantastic manuscript into an awesome novel.

[13] Shaun George of New Minas, Nova Scotia, for granting me the distinct privilege of using his photograph, *Lonesome Park*, as the cover image. You may view his online Flickr photos at https://www.flickr.com/photos/23641763@N08/

[14] André Richard of Memramcook, New Brunswick, for granting me the distinct privilege of using his photograph, *Evangeline at Grand Pré*, as the inside cover image. Do visit https://www.flickr.com/photos/andre_richard/2294311087/

[15] Douglas Mercer of Halifax, Nova Scotia, for granting me the distinct privilege of using his photograph, *Maman at Grand Pré*, as the key illustration for Chapter 13. Feel free to view this majestic and unforgettable bronze image online at https://www.flickr.com/photos/rexton/289899704/

[16] Nick Bunick, author of <u>In God's Truth</u>, for granting me the distinct privilege of using his commissioned portrait of Yeshua in the chapter entitled Messages for the 21st Century.

[17] Paula Bailey for granting me the distinct privilege of using her *Rose in Black and White* photograph in the chapter entitled Prayer of the Bodhisattva. Feel free to view this image at https://www.flickr.com/photos/auntiep/2262680/

Foreword

This book is a combination of [1] my passion for history, [2] my fascination with current DNA testing as it continues to prove and rewrite history as we have known it, [3] my intrigue with topics of a metaphysical nature, and [4] my French Acadian heritage.

In keeping, many hours were spent reading, researching and questioning these very topics of continued fascination. Truth be told, there were times when it felt as if I had traveled back in time to live, and love, among these ancestors of mine.

The voyage of July 4, 1632 was the first to the Acadian colony following the St. Germain-en-Laye treaty of March 29, 1632. By order of Cardinal Richelieu (Minister of State to King Louis XIII), Commander Isaac de Razilly came to re-occupy the colony. This was the same voyage that brought my direct ancestor, Germain Doucet, Sieur de LaVerdure, to these very shores.

According to Andrew Hill Clark in <u>Acadia: The Geography of Early Nova Scotia to 1760</u>, page 91, Razilly "sailed from France on July 4, 1632 in L'Espérance à Dieu, shepherding two transports, and disembarked some three hundred people (mostly men) and a variety of livestock, seeds, tools, implements, arms, munitions, and other supplies at La Have (La Hève, at the mouth of the La Have River in present Lunenburg County) on September 8."

Razilly was a cousin to Richelieu. One of the leaders of the Company of New France, he was both designated Lieutenant General of all the parts of New France, called Canada, as well as Governor of Acadie.

According to Sally Ross and Alphonse Deveau in <u>The Acadians of Nova Scotia: Past and Present</u>, page 16, it was in September that "Isaac de Razilly arrived in Acadia with three sailing vessels, 300 hand-picked men, three Capuchin Fathers and a few women and children."

Many of these early colonists later resettled at Port Royal.

The Acadian people were a group of hardy men and women who were willing to brave a new world for themselves and future generations. Prior to 1755, up to four generations had tilled the soil of Acadie.

The deportation of 1755 was a tragedy of epic proportions. During this upheaval, some families were torn asunder, many never to find each other again. Such has been forever immortalized by Longfellow's romantic epic poem entitled *Evangeline*.

Due to the crowded conditions on the ships, many lost their lives to the sickness and dysentery that raged rampant. As is usually the case, it was always the very young and the very old that were taken first.

Many of these transporters of human cargo were in poor shape. As a result, innocent lives were lost at sea beneath the waves.

The imprisoned Acadians were finally set free during the course of the 1760's.

To my way of thinking, however, all were imprisoned, not just those who were actually housed in prisons.

Finally allowed to settle in unoccupied areas of the Maritime Provinces, they began to rebuild their lost land of Acadie, proving, once again, to be the resourceful and resilient people they have always been.

Michele Doucette   December 24, 2008

In reflecting back on childhood memories, summers spent in rural Nova Scotia, on the farm belonging to my maternal grandparents, were the physical embodiment of the closest that I have ever come to experiencing "heaven" on earth.

Breakfast cooked on the old wood stove was my favorite part of the day. Granny would either cook me a hard-boiled egg with a soft, runny yolk or a bowl of porridge. To this day, I have never been able to perfect her uncanny ability to boil eggs in this fashion. As much as I continue to enjoy cooked oatmeal, I still relish the enhanced flavor of it having been cooked over a wood stove.

I loved to wander across the road so I could traverse the path down to the meadow beside the river. We called this area the intervale. Based on a dictionary definition, intervale means a low-lying tract of land along a river.

I would often sit, with book in hand, leaning against the old oak tree. This was also our favorite swimming spot.

As a child, I was a lover of solitude. I was a shy child, never truly sharing my innermost thoughts with anyone. Even though I was not one to say a great deal, I was one to think.

There were countless times, in fact, when I chose *not* to acknowledge the deeper thoughts that resided within. It was far easier to escape into a world of knights, castles, dragons, damsels in distress, fairies, leprechauns, queens, kings, princesses and the like.

I was always enchanted with the power of the written word, feeling their depths come alive within me, but mostly when I was alone. I am sure that all who know me would describe me thusly.

I often felt as if I never truly belonged to the era of my birth. Perhaps I had lived before, during the times that continued to fascinate and captivate me so.

My most favorite memories were of the times when my great grandmother would make the trip from Amherst to the farm.

The atmosphere was most relaxing and carefree, for it was during these visits that mother and daughter would converse solely in French.

I would sit and listen to the dialogue exchange for hours upon end. Time seemed that long to this wee slip of a girl. Needless to say, I was totally captivated by the language of my ancestors.

As a result of my fascination with books, history came to be a subject that I excelled in at school. Learning about my family history merely seemed an extension of what had come to pass within the walls of the classroom itself.

My maternal grandparents were wed on September 1, 1930. They honeymooned at Grand Pré.

Long intrigued with the pictures that were part of the family photo album, I knew that at one point in my life, I, too, would make the trek to Grand Pré. A premonition, if you will, it was something that I felt deep within my bones.

While in attendance at Acadia University in Wolfville, I was always much too involved with my Education studies to immerse myself within the local Acadian culture. All changed after graduation, however, when I was finally able to do that which I had always wanted to do.

At long last, I was able to completely dedicate myself to the reading and researching of Acadian history.

Not a seamstress by profession, I began to design a costume that I could wear while taking part in the summer Acadian celebrations at Grand Pré. This was not an easy task. There were many occasions when I was tempted to hire someone to finish the outfit for me. However, never having been a quitter, I prevailed until its completion, awkward fingers, countless pinpricks, and all.

It seemed as if I instinctively knew when it was time for me to pay Evangeline a visit. After having read Longfellow's contribution to Acadian history, I felt as if I knew her intimately.

I was twenty-five years old when I finally arrived at Grand Pré Historic Park, a day made even more special as it was the day before the celebration of my twenty-sixth birthday.

In keeping, Acadian Day, August 15, 2005, boasted music of the finest Acadian quality; dancers in Acadian costume; arts and crafts from local entrepreneurs; a variety of workshops featuring art and painting, dyke building and a treasure hunt (but without the use of a GPS device).

To tempt the taste buds, there were traditional Acadian dishes and other culinary treats.

I loved the corn soup, all the while thinking how easy it would be to make for myself.

The Clam Fricot was another popular choice.

Munching on the meat pie brought me back to Granny's homemade venison mincemeat pies sampled throughout the harsh winter months.

All was wonderful, save for a small sampling of Dandelion wine, offered only to adults of legal drinking age. I was unable to stomach the taste.

Acadians, and Acadians at heart, had eagerly gathered to have fun and celebrate together. Towards the end of the day, as festivities had drawn to a close, and most had already left the park grounds, I made one more quick visit to see Evangeline. After a day of wonderment and enjoyment, it seemed that she and I had made a deeper connection. Without knowing the why's of it all, I began to cry.

In an attempt to convey my emotional thoughts to her, I reached up to stroke the folds of her dress.

It was at that moment that I was overcome with a foreboding sense of dizziness and nausea, fainting at the base of the statue.

Chapter 1

Madeleine awoke to darkness, feeling most disoriented, reeling with what seemed like inner ear confusion. She tried to stand, only to fall back down.

"It's okay, Madeleine. You are going to be fine. Just take deep breaths. In, out. In, out. In, out."

This time when she attempted to sit upright, she was able to.

Thinking back to what had happened before fainting at the base of the Evangeline statue, she found it very strange that no one at the park had come to her assistance, even though there had been few people left, to see what was wrong.

She looked all around, trying to get her bearings.

Something didn't feel right. The air, although cool for what appeared to be a late summer evening, felt different. Not only did it feel different, it smelt crisp and clean, free of the twenty-first century smell, if there really was such a thing.

Madeleine simply sat, continuing to breathe deeply, until she felt able to stand.

Thank goodness she had excellent night vision. Didn't her mother always say that she was like a cat on the prowl after dark?

Finding her way to her feet, she took in her surroundings. The hair on her arms immediately stood up on end, and she experienced a deep chill to the bone, for there was no way that she could possibly still be at the park. Everything had disappeared from view, save a building close by, but how was that possible?

She quickly covered the short distance to the building, entering to discover what looked like a church. In no way, however, did this building resemble the church on the park grounds at Grand Pré.

There was nothing smooth to the touch about the wood. The metal handle positioned on the door reminded her of the type placed on the outhouse door at her grandparents' farm. As a result, she entered easily.

There were no pictures on the walls, no adornments of any kind. Madeleine found herself walking gingerly toward what seemed to resemble pews. Overcome with exhaustion, made even more intense by not knowing where she found herself, she sat down.

Reaching into her backpack, she quickly located the survival packet containing the blanket that always reminded her of a gigantic piece of aluminum foil. After positioning the pack as a pillow and tucking the blanket around and under, she lay down and proceeded to fall into a deep sleep.

Unbeknownst to Madeleine, someone had been watching and trailing her, not at all surprised by her appearance. It was as if she had been expected.

"She is the one," Madame Pêche whispered. Entering the church and quietly closing the door behind her, she, too, found her way to a pew; not to sleep, she was there to pray.

Madeleine was unsure of the time when she woke up. Rooting around in her backpack, she quickly located her watch. After pressing the Indiglo light, she noted the time to be 3:33 AM.

She smiled, further reassured that there would be some positive resolution to what was happening around her, as she had always been privy to these types of number combinations, with favorable results, all her life.

Wide awake, Madeleine stood up, wanting to explore the building that had become her haven. She was so startled to discover another person close by that she let out a shriek and fell back, cracking her head with a thud on the very pew that she had been sleeping on.

Within seconds, Madame Pêche was beside her. "Puis-je vous aider?"

"I am sorry, but …"

Madeleine searched for the words. In an effort to make the woman understand, she made another effort. "Je ne parle pas le français, madame."

The woman looked at her, puzzled. "Mais, vous parlez français maintenant. Êtes-vous anglais?"

Madeleine nodded her head, relieved that the woman was finally understanding. "Yes, I am English."

Madame Pêche began pacing back and forth, unsure how to proceed, for she, too, had a secret that had not been shared with the villagers. Madeleine had somehow stumbled across the sole woman in the village of Grand Pré who had the gift of being able to see into the future. Finally, she stopped pacing. She sat down and beckoned Madeleine closer.

"I have been expecting you," she shared in a whisper.

Madeleine was dumbfounded, for the very woman that had been chattering away in French, mere moments ago, was now speaking to her in English. The shock on her face was acknowledged by the woman with a tender smile.

"I speak both languages," said she.

"Who are you? Where am I? Why are we whispering?" asked Madeleine.

"I am known to the villagers of Grand Pré as Madame Pêche, although that is not my real name. Perhaps I can later share my name with you, but now is not the time. For now, however, I will tell you that I have been waiting, and watching, albeit secretly, for your arrival."

Madeleine was beginning to suspect that something was deeply wrong with Madame Pêche. Might this woman be suffering from Alzheimer's? She couldn't possibly be expecting someone from the future, could she? For the first time, Madeleine was beginning to feel fear coursing through her body.

"What year is it?" she asked in an unsure voice. She just felt an inner knowingness that something beyond all human reasoning was currently transpiring. Her intuition had never steered her wrong before, but there was definitely something otherworldly happening here, for lack of a better description.

"My dear child, it is August 16, 1754. Welcome to Grand Pré, Madeleine Sinclair."

Madeleine froze. "How is it that you know my name?" she demanded, roughly.

"Keep your voice down. Come with me to my house, and I shall tell you all that I know."

Madeleine's mind was a befuddled mess. How could this woman, whose name was yet to be revealed, know who she was? Further to that thought, could she trust her? If it really was 1754, she certainly had no choice but to follow her.

They walked, quickly and in complete silence, what seemed a few miles to the Pêche homestead. Closing the door behind her, Madeleine was quick to appreciate the warmth provided by the simple home. Turning to face Madame, she attempted a smile.

Madame indicated the bench near the table. "We can now talk more freely, Madeleine. Come. Sit."

Madeleine shivered, involuntarily.

"Would you like for me to put on a small fire? You must be chilled, having spent part of the night at the church."

"I thought I may have been in the Saint-Charles-des-Mines parish church, but I couldn't be sure."

"Yes, my dear. You quite know your Acadian history. After we have finished speaking, you shall know much more."

Madeleine, wondering what Madame Pêche meant by that comment, was sure, by now, that her emotions were running rampant across her face.

Madame laughed. "Yes, my dear, you are as easy to read as a book. Given the cards that life hands out to each of us, one must be able, at times, to maintain a stoic poker face."

Madeleine smiled, feeling a wee bit of déjà vu. "My mother is forever telling me the same thing, but I can never hide what I am feeling." Emotions quickly flickered across Madeleine's face as she thought of her mother who must, by now, be in a panic at not being able to reach her daughter.

"Do not worry about the time difference, Madeleine. The time you come from has merely been put on hold, waiting for your return."

"You told me back at the church that this is August 16, 1754. I have just come from August 15, 2005. How can one go back some 250 years in time? I do not understand."

"You are here because it is your destiny to be here. It is all part of the fabric of life, planned well before your birth on August 16, 1979. In your time, today would be your twenty-sixth birthday, am I right?"

Madeleine, still standing up to that point, collapsed in a heap on the hard mud floor. She began to cry. "How is it that you know so much about me?"

Madame Pêche lowered her body to the floor, drawing the shivering Madeleine into her arms, smoothing hair back from her face, over and over, much as a mother would in an effort to soothe her distraught child.

"Let me tell you a story."

And thus, it began.

"Sinclair, as you know, is a form of St. Clair. In Latin we say *Sanctus Clarus*. The name is said to mean 'Shining Light.' It seems that this shining light has become one of the biggest clues in the search for the real Holy Grail.

"The first St. Clair of your line, that is to say the first person to take the name, was Rollo the Viking, father of William Longsword.

"Your line then travels through many historic and important personages; namely, William de St. Clair, illegitimate son of Robert II de St. Clair, Duke of Normandy, who fought at Hastings in 1066, emerging victorious to become King William I of England; Henry I Sinclair, 1st Earl of Orkney, Baron of Roslin and Lord of Shetland, who traveled to the New World in 1398; as well as William Sinclair, 1st Earl of Caithness, grandson of Henry, who commissioned the building of Rosslyn Chapel in Scotland in 1446.

"Henry was a known patron of refugee Templars, a group that had been created by the kings of Jerusalem. These Templar Knights were deemed guardians of the Holy Grail.

"Much is emerging out of your time, Madeleine. There are many who now believe the Holy Grail to be "a code phrase describing the descendants of Jesus, the Holy Bloodline, that was a living vessel in which the Holy Blood was held, preserved, and perpetuated." [1] I am here to tell you that the Holy Grail was "spirited away from the doomed Montségur by three knights just a few days before the citadel surrendered" [2] in 1244.

"Cathar tradition suggests that the Holy Grail is actually a lineage of people descended from Jesus. If, indeed, "the scion of this Holy Bloodline were actually saved from Montségur, then these Holy Blood descendants, along with a fair number of Templar protectors, may well have ended up in Scotland with Henry Sinclair." [3] Based on your knowledge, you are now wondering if the descendants of Yeshua and Mary Magdalene could have been transported

---

[1] Mann, William F. (2004). *The Knights Templar in the New World: How Henry Sinclair Brought the Grail to Acadia* (p. xi). Rochester, VT: Destiny Books.
[2] Ibid.
[3] Mann, William F. (2004). *The Knights Templar in the New World: How Henry Sinclair Brought the Grail to Acadia* (p. xiii). Rochester, VT: Destiny Books.

here to Acadie. Let me just say that anything, and everything, is possible, my child."

Madeleine began to shiver in earnest. Madame Pêche stood up to gather the homespun blanket from the straw mattress. She quickly bundled it around Madeleine before continuing.

"Yours is a clan whose motto is *Commit thy work to God*, which is why you are here, although you know it naught at present." She paused for a brief moment, allowing Madeleine time to slowly digest the information.

"But what does all of this possibly have to do with why I am here in 1754?"

"You are the very first Sinclair female, born between 911 AD and 1979, who bears a very special birthmark. This birthmark looks like a Templar cross. That, in and of itself, makes you *the one*."

"Oh, my God!" Madeleine bolted upright. "How could you possibly know about my birthmark? I have always thought it the most ugly mark. If I am supposed to be *the one* as you propose, what am I supposed to do? What is my purpose?"

"Merely to reclaim that which has been lost all these years, sharing such with the world of your time."

Madeleine began shuddering anew at these solemn, yet profound and powerful words. Her emotions had run the full gamut and she was simply too exhausted to take in any more bewildering information.

"Come, Madeleine, it is time for you to rest. We will have much to discuss when you are feeling more refreshed."

Madeleine let Madame lead her to a straw mattress on the floor, close to the fireplace on the far right wall. Within moments, she was asleep.

Chapter 2

Madeleine awoke, momentarily disoriented, wondering why she was sleeping on such a hard mattress. Putting out her hand, she came in contact with what felt like a mud floor. She stretched her body, wondering why it felt so stiff and sore.

Suddenly, it all came flooding back in a torrential rush. She had somehow gone back in time to 1754, and it was her twenty-sixth birthday. She gave a most unladylike snort.

"I see you are remembering the circumstances wherein you currently find yourself, Madeleine. Do you find yourself well rested?"

Knowing that it could only be Madame Pêche speaking to her, she still jumped. "I'm sorry," she replied. "This is going to take some getting used to."

"Of course, my dear, of course. How are you feeling?"

"Much better, but I think that my body sorely disagrees."

Madeleine took her time getting up, stretching and flexing her muscles.

"Yes, I am sure that you are well accustomed to your box spring and mattress at home," Madame Pêche chuckled.

"How is it, Madame Pêche, that you are able to tell me so many things about my life and what I am accustomed to?"

"Are you familiar with the term clairvoyance, Madeleine?"

"Indeed, I am. A *clairvoyant* individual is someone who can acquire and access knowledge through paranormal sensory experiences, mainly by way of visions and pictures. Some people even refer to it as remote viewing. If someone has the ability to access information by way of feelings, we call this *clairsentience*. If you have the ability to hear things, you are deemed *clairaudient*. If someone has the ability to know something without knowing why, or how, they know it, they are *claircognizant*."

"Quite right, my dear. I gather that you are also interested in things of both a paranormal and metaphysical nature."

"Given my previous disclosure, that should have been easy to ascertain, especially for someone with your abilities," Madeleine chuckled. "While I believe that you are mainly clairvoyant, it would not surprise me at all if you were a culmination of all four."

Madame smiled, approvingly. "Again, you are right, my dear. You are most intuitively perceptive. Were you aware that you also have these same abilities?"

"I know for certain that I am clairsentient because I am completely governed by my feelings, soaking up everything around me like a sponge. The worst thing about being clairsentient is the negativity that seems to exude from people, from all types of media, especially newspapers and television. Trying to detach from this negativity continues to be my challenge. I do, however, remember the odd time or two when I just seemed to have that intuitive knowingness. The feeling was so strong, so right, so in keeping with my heart and not my head, that I just knew."

"Being the clairsentient individual that you are, Madeleine, you must learn to practice the art of emotional detachment.

Almost paradoxical, this detachment serves to make you a more compassionate and empathetic observer. So, too, do you have the ability to become more objective. In no way does this make one aloof and severe as some would seem to think, which is why it presents as a complete juxtaposition.

"This art of emotional detachment also enables one to better relate to the divine that exists within each soul, without their emotions running amuck; as Yeshua is oft paraphrased as saying, one must be of the world and yet not. Am I making any sense?"

"In truth, I am unsure how I feel about that at present and yet I have to somehow find the humor in the situation because I sincerely doubt that this is what Yeshua meant. I am beginning to surmise that the emotions I experienced in coming face to face with the bronze statue of Evangeline are what propelled me backwards in time. While I have always believed time travel to be plausible and possible, the fact that I am here, now, in 1754. This simply stupefies the mind and defies all human logic!"

"And that, dearest Madeleine, is the crux of the problem, for it has nothing to do with the human mind at all. Time travel is quite possible, as you have well proved here this day. Let us not belabor the point, shall we? What we need to do is come up with a credible story that I can share, as needed, with the villagers of Grand Pré, as to how you came to be here with me."

"What do the villagers have to say about your, umm, skills?"

Madeleine's innocent question garnered a hearty laugh from Madame Pêche. "I am both respected and feared. As well you know, Madeleine, people always fear what they do not know or have not experienced for themselves. They know that I am able to provide answers to the many questions that they leave me with, but they do not know that I have the ability to both see and visit the future."

Realization was beginning to dawn on Madeleine's face. "Ahhhh. So, that is how you know so much. We refer to that as astral travel. Have you ever journeyed to my time, to the twenty-first century?"

"In my visions, yes. If you are asking as to whether I have been there in the physical body, my answer is no, but purely because it has been my choice to remain here in physical embodiment. In my nightly astral travels, of course, I have been able to visit."

"And what do you think of my time?"

"After much astute observation, I can only conclude that the people there place too much emphasis on living a fast-paced life, one filled with stress. They do not live their lives filled with passion, with fun, with love, with laughter, with enjoyment, with spontaneity. Not only that, but how can you embrace the peace, the tranquility and the passion of the All That Is when you do not even make an effort to connect with the stillness within?"

"Yes, I quite agree with you Mother … er … Madame Pêche."

"Madeleine, dear, please feel free to call me Mother Pêche throughout the duration of your stay here. I shall do my best to mother you as my own."

"Do you have any children, Mother Pêche?"

"Yes, child, but they have long since departed."

"Meaning that …"

"The time they are from is not of this time."

"Which can only mean that you, too, have also traveled, like me, from a time, either before or after 1754."

Madame Pêche rewarded Madeleine with both a brief, albeit sad, smile as well as a knowing look.

"How did you get to be here? Have you been here a long time?"

"That, dear one, is a story for another time. When you are as old as I am, my child, time is always long, but then all we have is time, do we not?"

"Just knowing that you, too, are a relative stranger to the people here, I shant feel like such an outsider after all."

Madeleine heaved a sigh of relief that was extremely short lived due to the loud knock on the wooden door. Madame did her best to quickly reassure the frightened Madeleine before openly welcoming the visitor.

Chapter 3

"Âllo, Michel. How are you doing this delightful summer morning?"

"I am doing very well, as always, Mother Pêche, and you?"

Madeleine's ears perked up; she was most curious as to who was behind the door, also referring to Madame as Mother Pêche.

Madame invited Michel inside, quickly closing and latching the wooden door behind her. He was most surprised to come face to face with Madeleine. Wearing an outfit that was more colorful than typical Acadian wear, he immediately deduced that she was not from the area. He looked at Madame with a quizzical brow.

"Michel, I would like to introduce you to my young visitor. This is Madeleine Sinclair. She, too, has come from afar."

How could Mother Pêche have invalidated her trust so quickly? Madeleine did not want anyone to know that she was not from this time. Frightened anew by this particular exchange of words, Madeleine was quickly reassured with a hug from Madame.

"Michel is like my own son, coming by every morning, early, to take care of me and my needs before returning to help his own family with the remainder of their daily chores. A very special young man, he continues to keep the secrets that I have disclosed to him. He will do the same for you."

A knowing look and a nod passed between Michel and Madame. "Of that you can be sure, my good Mother."

Not really sure what to say, Madeleine gave Michel a timid smile.

"Come, Michel, sit. You, too, Madeleine. What I have to share concerns both of you."

It was bad enough waking up in 1754, but now Madeleine was really confused. How was it that what Madame had to share could possibly connect her with Michel? She barely knew him. Nothing was making any sense. Madeleine raised a hand to her throbbing temples, but the headache came upon her full force.

Realizing that she needed to lie down, she seemed to lose all sense of balance and began to fall, quickly succumbing to a dead faint. Caught by Michel, she was carried and gently lowered to the straw mattress on the floor.

"What is wrong, Mother Pêche?"

"Madeleine suffers from migraine headaches. Any amount of stress can trigger such severe pain that all she can do is lie down, completely enclosed in the dark, bless her soul. I fear that in all the excitement, I forgot to make mention of your stopping by this morning, so I am not surprised at this turn of events. All we can do is let her sleep, poor child."

Michel and Madame shared a compassionate look before sitting down to the table for a hearty breakfast of beans, potatoes, bread, butter and refreshing well water.

When Madeleine awoke, it was late afternoon; feeling groggy, she moaned and shifted her body ever so slightly, bit by bit, before raising herself to a seated position.

"How are you feeling, child?"

"While I have felt worse, sleeping on this straw mattress is not helping me overly much."

"Do you have any medication in your backpack, dear?"

"I think so." Madeleine looked around but was unable to locate her backpack anywhere. What she did see, however, was Madame rolling up the large homespun mat in order to reveal a cleverly hidden storage compartment in the floor.

"Just like my Granny's root cellar," she commented.

Mind you, upon further investigation, Madeleine was quick to conclude that this was not your ordinary root cellar, for several wooden stairs led down to a most sizeable mud packed area that seemed to lend itself to what looked like a tunnel of sorts. Madeleine did a double take. "Where does this lead, Mother Pêche?"

"That, my dearest, is part of the story that I shall be sharing with you and Michel, to be discussed at another time. For now, I will just go down these stairs to retrieve your bag."

Knowing that the backpack would have needed to be placed out of sight, Madeleine was concerned. "This seems too difficult for you to be at, my good Mother. Are you sure there is not an easier hiding spot to be had?"

"Well there may be, but there's danger afoot. I suspect we have a year at most, or conceivably less. Time is not always cooperative with exact dates, dearest Madeleine. It is probably best for us to get into the habit of using this space now. It is also helpful that my house is the farthest one away from the village itself."

"Why is it that you live so far away?"

"This home had once belonged to the healer of the village; when I arrived, it was abandoned. After deciding it to be the best possible abode, I chose to stay.

"What you also need to remember is that while many of the folk here are an extremely superstitious lot, you, Michel and I are not." She paused a moment. "Come now, Madeleine. You need to take your medication. You also need to eat. We will talk more after you have eaten and are feeling better."

Knowing that it was pointless to argue with someone who appeared to know everything that there was to know about her, Madeleine simply nodded in agreement, giving a weary sigh. With a full stomach, she knew that she would feel better. This, then, would also allow the medication to do its job, further inducing her to sleep. Considering how far she had come in such a short time, clearly she needed the rest.

Chapter 4

Madeleine was ready for the knock on the door the next morning. Taking a quick look at her watch, while making sure that it also remained hidden, she could see that it was 8:00 AM. The medication had done its job and she felt incredibly well rested.

Madame had previously disclosed to her that Michel arose at 4:00 AM every morning in order to begin his day. He always arrived at about 8:00 AM to break his fast with her.

The table, this morning, was set with bread, butter, eggs, potatoes and apple cider.

Theirs was a routine that serviced them both, one that was demonstrated by their complete familiarity and ease with one another. Michel would then spend several hours with Madame before returning home by noon, working straight through into the early evening.

At Madame's there was a small garden that needed tending. She had one cow that needed milking every morning. In addition, there were two dozen chickens that afforded her with eggs aplenty to sell to the villagers. At times, she would also barter for other items.

Since her introduction to the village, Michel had always been her go-between. Rarely would she be graced with a visit from someone other than Michel, but then she liked it that way.

On this particular morning, Michel had taken extra care with his appearance before heading the few miles to be with Mother Pêche. All the while, his thoughts kept returning to Madeleine.

Even though they had just met, and briefly at that, there was something about her that made his heart sing, giving him that extra lift in his step. While he seemed to discern that she was also an intuitive individual, he found that he was quite surprised by this immediate reaction.

What was so uncanny was that Madeleine, out of the blue, had turned up much like Madame.

He had always wandered away from the village, coming to the long abandoned homestead to think. Eight years ago, a mere lad of eighteen, he had been the one to find Madame sitting at the base of the largest tree on the property.

For some strange reason, he was not the least bit surprised to find her there. It felt as if he had been expecting her, as surreal as it was.

They quickly struck up a conversation that, unbeknownst to either of them, was to lead to the familial like relationship they now shared.

Michel was a most compassionate soul. Living his life by the Golden Rule meant that he treated others with love, acceptance and respect. Believing in peace and unity of peoples, he was always the mediator between friends.

He always enjoyed his time with Mother Pêche, learning much about life, learning much about himself. Sensing that he was about to become involved in something of major significance, and knowing naught what to expect, he was not afraid. He both knew and felt that one had the power to make their life that which they wanted it to be. With that belief in mind, he had always been one to embrace change.

Mother Pêche was waiting outside for him, greeting him with a smile and a hug. "Come in, come in, Michel. It is always a pleasure to break my fast with you on mornings such as these." Mother Pêche entered first.

Madeleine was there to greet him with a radiant smile as well. He felt such warmth and happiness flood his very being that he missed his footing, stumbling in through the door. He looked up with a sheepish grin. Mother Pêche gave a most gleeful laugh and was unable to stop. Soon they were all laughing and holding their sides.

"I have always said that laughter is good for the soul. Thank you for such a delightful gift this day, my Michel. Let us now break our fast amidst marvelous company."

Over breakfast, Madeleine learned that Michel *dit Sophie* was the oldest (at age twenty-six) of ten children, born to Honoré LeBlanc and Geneviève Baillon, followed by René (twenty-three), Pierre (twenty-one), Claude (nineteen), Sophie (seventeen), Charlotte Anne (fifteen), Philippe (thirteen), Joseph (eight), Cécile (six) and Madeleine (three).

"How wonderful to be part of such a large family, Michel. Although we are the same age, both twenty-six, I am an only child. My parents, unable to have any more children, waited a long time for me. It must be so busy in your house."

"Indeed it is, mam'selle, indeed it is, but that is what makes it so enjoyable. I must say that I have never been lonely. How about you? Did you find it lonely growing up?"

Mother Pêche patted Madeleine's hand reassuringly. "While being an only child is not without its solitary moments, it does not have to be lonely, does it, Madeleine?"

Madeleine turned to Mother Pêche with a grateful smile before refocusing on Michel.

"I have learned a great deal about myself, being an only child, but I have never felt that I was truly alone. When I am communing with nature, I am able to connect with the trees, the plants, the stars, the animals and the birds in such a way that I feel truly alive. Even the rocks and special stones share their energies with me.

"I love children and hope to be able to raise a sizeable family. I want to live in the country where I can teach my children to appreciate the peace that is to be found within when one fully interrelates with nature. I want them to appreciate life, becoming one with the moment. I want them to live and be happy with who they are."

Madeleine's eyes shone with the sparkle of her heartfelt wishes. As Michel continued to listen to Madeleine speak with such zeal, with such fervor, with such passion, his own smile continued to grow.

"I thank you so much for sharing this with me, mam'selle. I agree with all that you have shared, for I, too, feel the same way.

"I find nature to be invigorating and rejuvenating. How could it be otherwise when nature is where the Creator resides, yes?" Looking at Mother Pêche, he continued. "But for now, you must excuse me, as I have chores to attend to."

Arising from the table, he bowed to both women before unlatching the door and closing it behind him.

Mother Pêche sat for a moment, taking in Madeleine's flushed face with a bemused look on her own, to which Madeleine responded, "Why are you looking at me like that?"

Mother Pêche just snorted. "Let us tidy up these dishes, dear one, so that you and I can relax and further discuss my role in this most interesting scenario."

Chapter 5

The remainder of the afternoon passed in what could only be described as one of total astoundment. Having arrived at Grand Pré in what would be considered rather dubious circumstances, both women were time travelers.

"Ah, Madeleine, now to begin telling you about my story. As you know, based on what Michel has shared, it was 1746 when I came to be here in Grand Pré. I know that you will believe what I am about to share, for you have come from the future.

"By comparison, I arrived here from the past, with a fairly significant history, from the time of the Knights Templar, to be precise. Known as Jacques de Molay, I have traveled a considerable distance to be here with you."

Madeleine drew in a sharp, quick breath. Goosebumps arose on her flesh. The hair on her arms stood completely upright, as if at command.

She'd *always* resonated with the Knights Templar, the Holy Grail, the Holy Bloodline union of Yeshua and Mary Magdalene, the legendary Merovingian kings, Montségur, the Cathars, the treasure of King Solomon, Rennes-le-Château, Rosslyn Chapel, Gnosticism, the principality of the Languedoc region of southern France.

In keeping with the DNA and archaeological findings of her time, Madeleine could go on and on and on. This *had* to be why she'd been propelled here. She began to shiver uncontrollably. Mother Pêche draped a woolen blanket around her with understanding, care and concern.

"Does Michel know any of what you are about to share with me?"

"While there are many things that I have not yet revealed, I have taken the time to share things pertinent to his central ancestor, Bertrand de Blanchefort, Grand Master of the Knights Templar from 1156 to 1169. Without disclosing my identity, Michel sees me as a historian of a sort.

"He knows that I have come to his time, courtesy of the past, just as you have come to his time, albeit from the future. This is quite the tangled web of time that has been created, yes?"

Madeleine found herself offering an acknowledging smile.

"I have also taken the time to share the metaphysical and spiritual factors akin to my life in France, for that was what he needed to know. But it is with you, dearest one, that I must share my complete and unedited story, given that it is your Sinclair line that was to become intertwined with my own, whilst in service to the Knights Templar.

"First and foremost, let it be said that I am *not* here to disclose and discuss the nature of my upcoming arrest at the hands of King Philippe IV and Pope Clement V. As well you know, the king was hugely in debt to our organization. Up until that time, we were answerable only to the Pope, but Philippe managed to use his influence to demobilize the organization, all in an attempt to destroy us. Alas, I digress, for I am but here to share my knowledge as the last documented Grand Master."

Mother Pêche paused, taking a deep breath before resuming. "Are you ready? Shall we begin?"

All Madeleine could do was mutely nod her head in the affirmative.

"Madeleine, I know that you are well familiar with the events at Montségur in March 1244. In fact, I know that it is one of your deepest wishes to visit this last Cathari stronghold in the Languedoc area of the Midi-Pyrénées, and for good reason, as you shall soon discover."

Madeleine gave a confirmatory nod.

"Were you also aware that several knights managed to escape with the reputed treasure, under the cover of total darkness, mere days prior to the surrender of the fortress?"

Madeleine smiled knowingly before answering. "Although the nature of this treasure has never been identified, probably because it has never been found, I knew, and felt, that they were to have possessed something of immense value. There has been much speculation that it consisted of the Holy Grail, whatever that might have been. I took the final surrender at Montségur to mean that all of the Cathars were burned together at the base of the mountain."

"Madeleine, I am here to tell you about the Cathari treasure that was secreted away, down the mountain and across the French crusade lines; a treasure that was most valuable and still is."

Still is, Madeleine thought within the very recesses of her mind. "You mean it still exists? How can we access it? What is it?"

Madeleine started to rise from her seat. Mother Pêche just smiled her secretive smile before beckoning her to remain seated. "The treasure, dear one, was actually tri-fold in nature. Let me begin by saying that Yeshua had *two* wives, a most acceptable position for a Jewish Rabbi of his day. He was married to Miriam (of Bethany of the House of Saul) [4] as has been clearly alluded to in the Bible."

---

[4] Montgomery, Hugh. (2006). *The God-Kings of Europe: The Descendants of Jesus Traced Through the Odonic and Davidic Dynasties* (p. 32). San Diego, CA: The Book Tree.

Mother Pêche deliberately paused for theatrical emphasis before continuing.

"Things have a tendency to get a tad murky once Mirium (of the House of Æthiopia) known as Magdalene [5] is added to the equation, for, you see, she was his second companion. Whilst both were strong and prominent women, for some reason the writers and compilers of the Bible have been trying to keep this covered up for a very long time."

Madeleine was mesmerized by this unexpected turn of events, knowing that there was more to come.

The intense feeling that she was now experiencing was akin to someone sitting on the very edge of their seat, just waiting for it to let loose, ready for the plummeting fall. She took several deep breaths, attempting to calm her wildly beating heart, unsure as to where this might be going and how it could even possibly relate to the situation at hand.

---

[5] Montgomery, Hugh. (2006). *The God-Kings of Europe: The Descendants of Jesus Traced Through the Odonic and Davidic Dynasties* (p. 32). San Diego, CA: The Book Tree.

"The Cathari treasure that was secreted down the mountain at Montségur was [1] a direct female descendant of the Elchasai line, courtesy of Miriam of Bethany, [2] a direct female descendant connected with the Æthiopian line, courtesy of Mirium Magdalene, and [3] a copy of a book, a codex actually, written by Yeshua himself. All were transported safely, and discreetly, to the isle of Scotland. Hence, we have the tripartite nature of the treasure itself."

"I still do not follow you, my good Mother. How does this treasure actually connect with my family?"

"My answer to this, your question, Madeleine, first begins with Michel. One of the knights in question, entrusted with the safe keeping of the treasure, was a direct line male descendant of Bertrand de Blanchefort, the sixth Grand Master of the Knights Templar.

"Bertrand was a Cathar who had to practice his faith in secret. He was also the same Grand Master responsible for what would become the traditional seal depicting two knights on one horse, a seal around which there has been, and continues to be, much discourse."

Mother Pêche rose, walking about the room for a moment before resuming her seated position at the table.

"Bertrand de Blanchefort, in turn, was a direct male descendant (father to son to son to son) of King Clovis I, a Merovingian king. The Merovingians, it is said, wore their hair long, had a birthmark between their shoulder blades which resembled what later came to be called a Templar cross, and possessed magical powers. Michel bears this same birthmark, but upon his right breast."

Madeleine gasped in total shock, knowing that she bore the exact same mark above her left breast. How uncanny that they should both bear the same birthmark. What did it mean? "My good Mother, this is just so much to take in, and yet I am able to follow you with considerable ease."

"So now you are able to see why I could only share so much with Michel. Eventually, it will be up to you, should you choose, to share all of this with him, given your knowledge on these very topics that one might deem esoteric."

Madeleine responded by nodding.

"Let us now attempt to make the final connection for you, shall we?

"Both knights traveled with the treasure to Scotland, finding refuge with the Sinclair family. The de Blanchefort knight married the direct female descendant connected with the Æthiopian alliance. It is their very blood which courses through the veins of your new young friend, Michel *dit Sophie* LeBlanc.

"You must also remember, dearest Madeleine, that long has your family been noted as being the protectors of the Holy Grail; such was further accomplished when the Sinclair line. courtesy of a marital alliance, merged with the direct female *Elchasai* descendant of Miriam of Bethany, the one who carried a title meaning *Higher Power*. It is her blood that courses through your veins.

"So you see, dear heart, both you and Michel are direct descendants of Yeshua."

Madeleine simply stared at the old woman before her. While unafraid of the position that she was now finding herself in, she knew that this was going to take many days to absorb.

"To conclude, dearest Madeleine, the new metaphysical equation is simply this; your Sinclair line, meaning *Shining Light*, added to Michel's LeBlanc (de Blanchefort) line, meaning *House of Light* or *Fortress of Light*, is the much needed merger to bring back that which was once lost to the world. In order to complete this mission, you must both return to your time in the twenty-first century world."

After pausing for emphasis, Mother Pêche continued.

"While there is a wee bit more to be added to this story, I feel it best to leave it for now. In the meantime, ponder and reflect upon what I have shared with you, knowing that Michel does not have access to this knowledge. I will next share with you that which he knows, but first I must take a walk outside."

While Mother Pêche walked about, trying to loosen up from the stiffness of sitting so long on the wooden benches, Madeleine chose to walk about the interior of the house.

As promised, she resumed her story the moment she returned.

"Michel knows that he is the direct descendant of both Bertrand de Blanchefort as well as the de Blanchefort knight who was key in secreting the Cathari treasure away in 1244. He knows that the treasure was taken to Scotland, although he knows naught what this treasure is.

"I have spoken with him at great length about the Cathars. While he does not know that I have come as Jacques de Molay, he does know that I have come as a Knights Templar brother, so he has some understanding of our organization.

"I have also delved into the topic of reincarnation, but he knows nothing about the theory of quantum travel."

"Mother, I have but one nagging question. Would not our coming together, should that be the result, be seen as familial incest?"

Madeleine was squirming on her stool, clearly most uncomfortable at having posed this possibility.

In an attempt to put her at ease, Mother Pêche smiled most reassuringly. "My dearest child, do you not remember the converging of royal lines in ancient Egypt, whereby brothers married their sisters and half-sisters, in order to inherit the throne as pharaoh? It was always the female line through which the right to rule was passed.

"While ancestors of your lines have continued to intermarry in order to keep the sanctity of the bloodlines pure, they have also added new blood every few generations. So, while you and Michel are both direct descendants of the Holy Bloodline, your conjoining would not be that of a close cousin. There would be no need to seek dispensation from the church in order to marry.

"While royalty has long married cousins, all in an attempt to maintain the purity of their lines, much like the ancient pharaohs, we did not understand the genetics of such unions. Based on what I have shared with you here, however, you need not worry."

Madeleine relaxed somewhat, smiling back at Madame.

"Let it also be known, Madeleine, that while I will never make any claim to be able to forecast future events, I am only here to better prepare you both for your place in it. And that, dear one, is more than enough for today."

Following a simple supper fare of bread and butter, both women settled down for a much needed rest, knowing that morning would arrive soon enough with Michel on their very threshold.

Chapter 6

Each morning thereafter proceeded exactly like the one before, save for Mother Pêche sharing more metaphysical knowledge with both Michel and Madeleine when she could. In addition, there were countless discussions in keeping with the true teachings of Yeshua.

Mother Pêche also spoke about the force (energy) behind thought and intent, in that being shaped by our thoughts, we become what we think. Simply put, "what you think about is where your energy goes. Put another way, energy moves to whatever your consciousness focuses on." [6]

Madeleine was a firm believer in maintaining her own power. Knowing that she was responsible for whatever she created, she always made a conscious effort to watch what she was thinking and to monitor what she was saying, all in

---

[6] Sharp, Michael. (2004). *Dossier of The Ascension: A Practical Guide to Kundalini Activation* (p. 60). St. Albert, AB: Avatar Publications.

an attempt to make sure that she never intentionally gave her power away.

Given that there were but two choices, meaning that one could either maintain conscious control or unconscious control over their lives, she always chose the former.

Each individual is the source of their own energy. That having been said, each individual has their own energy signature as well.

While many people have little understanding of the power that they wield (or not, should that also be their choice), it is true that "the more you are interested in something, the more you think about it, and the more you focus intent on it, the closer you are to that thing. The less you think about something, then the farther you are away from it." [7]

Being the creator of your life, this means, in essence, that you can manifest something into your life with continued

---

[7] Sharp, Michael. (2004). *Dossier of The Ascension: A Practical Guide to Kundalini Activation* (p. 63). St. Albert, AB: Avatar Publications.

and concentrated effort, because energy always follows intent.

Albeit not from this time, Mother Pêche had learned much about the French Acadian culture from Michel.

As a result, she was quite eager to pass this knowledge and understanding along to Madeleine, these people being the younger woman's ancestors, as she would need to learn to blend in with the people here so as not to appear overly conspicuous; one never knew how long one's stay was needed.

It was also Madeleine's intent that she learn as much as possible about life in 1754. Who would have thought that she would be in a position to become inspired by the very fact that her personal genealogical research was meeting up with actual history?

While the life here was not an easy one, for the people worked long, exhaustive days, the tranquility was what resonated deep within Madeleine's soul.

The Mi'kmaq of the area had long since befriended the French Acadian populace, sharing much of their ways and their knowledge upon the settlers' arrival to this new land. They had since remained friends for a great many years.

Both peoples believed and adhered to the principles of neutrality and taking only what was needed. In turn, Mother Earth was deeply respected. Madeleine had also known that the French Acadian people of this time were mostly farmers.

In 1632, Sieur Isaac de Razilly was appointed Lieutenant General of Acadie by his cousin, Cardinal Richelieu.

A "man of more than ordinary ability, of keen insight and affable manners" [8] as per Samuel de Champlain, he founded a settlement at La Hève.

"Among the people he brought over from France were tenant farmers from inland agricultural areas like Poitou and others from places on the coast of France such as

---

[8] Canadian Genealogy Resources. (2008). *The Founders of Acadie* accessed on November 15, 2008 at www.canadiangenealogy.net/chronicles/founders_acadia.htm

Saint-Onge and Aunis. The settlers numbered about 300 men and 12 to 15 women." [9]

It appears that de Razilly, born among the French nobility, came with a vision to people this new land, with every succeeding year, bringing as many people here as he could.

Upon the death of de Razilly in 1635, he was succeeded by Charles de Menou, seigneur d'Aulnay de Charnisay. It was d'Aulnay who moved the settlers to Port Royal, setting up new homesteads on ideal marshland.

This is where "the seedlings of the French Acadian population and culture were to take root." [10] An ideal spot, Port Royal boasted "good farming land … within reasonable sailing distance to the largest rivers in the northeast." [11]

---

[9] Archaeology in Nova Scotia. (2002). *Info Sheet – The Acadians 1* accessed on November 15, 2008 at
http://monumentleblanc.com/images/infoaca1.pdf

[10] Landry, Peter. (2008). *History of Nova Scotia: Book 1, Chapter 7: The deRazilly Settlement at LeHeve* accessed on November 15, 2008 at www.blupete.com/Hist/NovaScotiaBk1/Part1/Ch07.htm

[11] Landry, Peter. (2008). *History of Nova Scotia: Book 1, Chapter 8: The Battling Barons of Acadia* accessed on November 15, 2008 at www.blupete.com/Hist/NovaScotiaBk1/Part1/Ch08.htm

The marshlands of the area were "large, treeless, stone-free plains that were well suited to farming." [12] It was most fortunate that there were people amongst this entourage who "recognized the agricultural potential of the tidal salt marshes," [13] having already been familiar with similar methods of dyking practiced in France.

The new settlers moved quickly "to build dykes along the outer marsh areas. Sometimes these dykes were built by driving five or six rows of logs into the ground, laying other logs one on top of the other between these rows, filling all the spaces between the logs with well packed clay and then covering everything over with sods cut from the marsh itself. Sometimes dykes were built by simply laying marsh sods over mounds of earth." [14]

---

[12] Archaeology in Nova Scotia. (2002). *Info Sheet – The Acadians 1* accessed on November 15, 2008 at monumentleblanc.com/images/infoaca1.pdf

[13] Archaeology in Nova Scotia. (2002). *Info Sheet – The Acadians 2* accessed on November 15, 2008 at monumentleblanc.com/images/infoaca2.pdf

[14] Ibid.

They also cleverly devised "a system of drainage ditches combined with an ingenious one-way water gate called an *aboiteau* … a hinged valve in the dyke which allowed fresh water to run off the marshes at low tide, but which prevented salt water from flowing onto the dyked farmland as the tide rose." [15]

They would then wait between two and four years, as such was the length of time needed for the salt from the marshes to be washed away by snow and rain. Thereafter, they were left with fertile soil that yielded most abundant crops (wheat, oats, barley, rye, peas, corn, flax, hemp), in addition to their gardens (beets, carrots, parsnips, onions, chives, shallots, herbs, salad greens, cabbages, turnips, potatoes).

They made considerable use of the coarse salt-marsh hay, called spartina, "that grew naturally even when the marshes were covered twice daily by the tides. Their use of this hay proved to be very important for the stability and self-sufficiency of their communities … maintaining large

---

[15] Archaeology in Nova Scotia. (2002). *Info Sheet – The Acadians 2* accessed on November 15, 2008 at monumentleb-lanc.com/images/infoaca2.pdf

numbers of cattle throughout the winter months" [16] mainly for milk, working animals and trade purposes. Pigs roamed rather freely, providing them with pork. Chickens were kept primarily for eggs. They supplanted "what they produced on their small farms by hunting and fishing. They even brewed their own spruce and fir beer." [17]

Madeleine was amazed at both the ingenuity as well as the self-sufficiency of Michel's people, establishing trade with New England for items such as "molasses, cooking pots, board axes, clay pipes, gunpowder, fabrics and rum," [18] while also trading "grain from the fertile marshlands, cattle well-fed on salt-marsh hay, and furs they had obtained from trapping and trade with the Mi'kmaq." [19] In addition, they also managed to acquire "cottons, thread, lace, firearms and

---

[16] Archaeology in Nova Scotia. (2002). *Info Sheet – The Acadians 2* accessed on November 15, 2008 at monumentleblanc.com/images/infoaca2.pdf
[17] Ibid.
[18] Archaeology in Nova Scotia. (2002). *Info Sheet – The Acadians 1* accessed on November 15, 2008 at monumentleblanc.com/images/infoaca1.pdf
[19] Ibid.

religious items from France" [20] through their French comrades at Louisbourg.

Madeleine was quickly taken back to the time when she had visited Fortress Louisbourg on Cape Breton Island as a young teen. She had made the mistake of wearing a red shirt on the day in question, and the French garrison soldiers (actors on site) had given her a rough time for siding with the enemy (none other than the British). Thank goodness she had remembered to stay away from all red fabrics while sewing her Acadian outfit.

The French Acadian people were very much community oriented, performing many tasks together. They clearly recognized and understood that their strength lay in assisting each other.

First and foremost, it was absolutely essential that the dykes be maintained. They would also gather to clear land and build a house for a young couple who had married, this

---

[20] Archaeology in Nova Scotia. (2002). *Info Sheet – The Acadians 1* accessed on November 15, 2008 at monumentleblanc.com/images/infoaca1.pdf

special activity quickly becoming "an occasion for work, fun, food and celebration," [21] with music being provided with fiddles and jaw harps.

The men were primarily responsible for repairing the dykes each spring. In addition, they also kept building new dykes in order to gain more land.

Crops were planted in the spring of the year and harvested in late summer and early fall. The sheep were sheared in the warm days of summer. After the harvest was gathered, some of the hogs and sheep were killed; this meat was salted for the winter months.

Over the winter, the men and older boys cut firewood and timber in the woods, making simple tables, chairs, beds, cradles and sideboards. They fished, hunted and trapped, also making the family's footwear, be they wooden shoes

---

[21] Archaeology in Nova Scotia. (2002). *Info Sheet – The Acadians 1* accessed on November 15, 2008 at monumentleblanc.com/images/infoaca1.pdf

(*sabots*), as were typically worn in France, or aboriginal moccasins.

The women were responsible for the household chores. They kept the fire lit, cooking all the meals. They worked at preserving the food. They made the family's clothes and did the laundry. They milked the cows, gathered the eggs and tended to their vegetable gardens. They also supervised the apple and pear orchards.

Throughout the winter months, they would card, spin and weave wool for clothing items and blankets. They knit socks and stockings. Both the hemp and the flax were woven into linen for clothes.

Their homes were built in the French construction manner known as *charpente*, the house being "a substantial wood framed structure on a basalt fieldstone foundation. A massive hearth, oven and chimney stood at one end of a single room. The walls were partly filled with clay and the roof was thatched." [22]

"The base and exterior walls of the [circular] oven [and fireplace complex] were made of the same field stones used in the foundation of the house, and it seems to have been lined with clay. The oven door was probably at the back of the fireplace, inside the house." [23]

Madeleine continued to be amazed by the fortitude and independence of these resourceful and resilient people.

Dan Brown's spiritual thriller, The Da Vinci Code, was first released in 2003. Madeleine disclosed to Mother Pêche that it was the reading of this very text that had initially spurred her to investigate the Knights Templar. She'd even taken the time to visit Rosslyn Chapel in Scotland.

---

[22] The Girouard Family Site. *A Sample Home in Acadia* accessed on November 15, 2008 at www.girouard.org/cgi-bin/page.pl?file=acadian_home&n=4

[23] Archaeology in Nova Scotia. (2002). *Info Sheet – The Acadians 3* accessed on November 15, 2008 at monumentleblanc.com/images/infoaca3.pdf

Madeleine knew about Henry I Sinclair (Earl of Orkney) having traveled to these very shores, also befriending the Mi'kmaq peoples. What she found even more fascinating, however, was the fact that current Y-DNA testing results of the twenty-first century were showing this to be true.

According to the St. Clair DNA Research Project, [24] there is an aboriginal male, living in Canada, whose test result showed him as being of the same haplogroup (R1b1) as other male Sinclair (St. Clair) individuals whose documented lineage could be traced directly back to Henry I Sinclair; remembering, of course, that Y-DNA is only passed from father to son.

Without a doubt, DNA testing was the science that was beginning to prove and rewrite history as had been previously known to the multitude.

By the same token, one could not lose sight of mtDNA testing.

---

[24] St. Clair Research. (2006). *Sinclair/St. Clair DNA Research Project* located at http://www.stclairresearch.com

In keeping with the founding mothers of Acadie, Madeleine was able to remember visiting the website of Lucie LeBlanc Consentino [25] for proven mtDNA test results.

Deliberating on this mtDNA knowledge made Madeleine realize that there was something about the word Æthiopia as attached to Mirium Magdalene, but what was it?

Keep focused, Madeleine, keep focused.

After much intense concentration, it came to her. Professor Hugh Montgomery had written that Æthiopia had nothing to do with the modern country called Ethiopia. Instead, it was "Greek for *the land of the burnt-face people* and was used for any dark-skinned person, but particularly for the Arabian Semites or Nabateans (or Sabateans), whose territory surrounded the Tetrachy of Herod, with their capital in Petra. Historically, the Bible called them the Edomites." [26]

---

[25] Consentino, Lucie LeBlanc. (1998). *Acadian & French Ancestral Home* located at www.acadian-home.org/frames.html
[26] Montgomery, Hugh. (2006). *The God-Kings of Europe: The Descendants of Jesus Traced Through the Odonic and Davidic Dynasties* (p. 31). San Diego, CA: The Book Tree.

It was Madeleine's guess that too many people were looking for evidence of this second wife in all the wrong places.

In keeping with Miriam of Bethany, there were some rather interesting remarks, for it was the descendants of this line that had been denoted as being the Elchasai. Accordingly, "the Elchasaites were an early Judaic-Christian sect who were also called *Mughtasilab* by al-Nadim and *Katharioi* (from which we get the name Cathar) in the Manicheaen work, *Kephalaia*." [27]

Clearly, these ancestors of hers *were* the forerunners of the Cathars.

---

[27] Montgomery, Hugh. (2006). *The God-Kings of Europe: The Descendants of Jesus Traced Through the Odonic and Davidic Dynasties* (p. 34). San Diego, CA: The Book Tree.

Chapter 7

Madeleine knew that she had to make the most of her time in 1754, however long that turned out to be.

A believer in synchronicity, she continued to reassure herself that she was meant to be here, that she had been destined to meet Mother Pêche, that she was meant to learn of her special heritage.

She was still having a hard time accepting that she and Michel were meant to be the forerunners of something monumental, something of extraordinary proportion, that was destined to unfold back within her time period of the twenty-first century, if, indeed, they were able to return.

Knowing the difficulty that she was experiencing, all in an attempt to grapple with the knowledge as presented by Mother Pêche, she could not help but wonder how Michel was going to feel about all of this.

How were they going to explain this happenstance to him?

Would he even be willing to participate?

While it was true that Mother Pêche and Michel had built a solid relationship over the past eight years, she had also been grooming him, imparting much in the way of metaphysical knowledge over the course of their time together, for what was to be, for what was to become.

This knowingness caused Madeleine to reflect upon the works of Sir Frances Bacon in his penmanship as William Shakespeare, for he, too, had been setting the stage, had he not?

In any case, she was now living in Michel's time. That having been said, she was learning to make the best of it.

It was pointless to worry, especially as Mother Pêche did assure her that time in the twenty-first century was standing still, awaiting her return.

A believer in past lives, she had since become a believer in future lives. Might this mean that parallel lives were also possible?

Knowing that time was not linear, Madeleine knew that she had to continue to believe and trust.

With this in mind, following Michel's departure at midday the next afternoon, Madeleine asked Mother Pêche if she could teach her how to card, spin and weave wool, knowing that this would also afford much relief for aged fingers.

She remembered reading that Grand Pré had been touted as being the "quiet metropolis of the Acadian people." [28]

With Grand Pré being a major center of its day, bolts of cloth were often imported from both Louisbourg and New England for the making of clothes. Mind you, they were still wearing woolen stockings.

Eureka. Finally there was something she could assist with, something she could learn as an aside, a means of earning her keep.

---

[28] Roberts, Charles G.D. (1898). *A Sister to Evangeline: Being the Story of Yvonne de Lamourie, and How She Went Into Exile with the Villagers of Grand-Pré* (p. 2). New York, NY: Lamson, Wolffe and Company.

In addition to the relationship that had already begun to form between the two women, Madeleine was eager to enter into this new apprenticeship relationship with Mother Pêche, one of total respect and acceptance for the skills she would gladly share.

The purpose for the carding of wool, a most time consuming task, was to straighten and separate the wool fibers, making them easier to spin into yarn.

First off, the wool had to be picked clean of sticks and burrs. Next, the wool was boiled in order to clean it. Then it was set out to dry in the sun. After that, it was teased so that it would be easier to card with the carding combs. This was done by pulling it apart with quick side-to-side movements, until it almost resembled the look of a cloud.

Next came the carding. [29] Used in pairs, the carding combs were wooden paddles with teeth made from wire. Wool was

---

[29] Wonder How To, Inc. (2008). *How to card wool for spinning by making rolags* accessed on November 15, 2008 at https://weaving.wonderhowto.com/how-to/card-wool-for-spinning-by-making-rolags-251603/

repeatedly combed from one card to the other, until all of the fibers were straight and fluffy, thereby strengthening the wool in the process. Once the carding was finished, the fiber was rolled off the card into a long roll for spinning, the finished product being soft, fluffy wool, for such made spinning easier.

Lastly, the fluffy wool was spun into yarn [30] for knitting. Considering that Madeleine had learned to knit as a young girl, the rest was going to be a breeze. Not only that, but she was inheriting skills to take back with her.

On top of these newly acquired skills, Mother Pêche also taught Madeleine how to weave cloth from flax. Madeleine had absolutely no idea that linen came from flax and that it was the strongest of vegetable fibers, having two to three times the strength of cotton. It became even more interesting when Mother Pêche further explained that flax was considered to be the oldest fiber used for clothing purposes.

---

[30] Wonder How To, Inc. (2008). *How to hand spin wool using the woolen long draw* accessed on November 15, 2008 at https://weaving.wonderhowto.com/how-to/hand-spin-wool-using-woolen-long-draw-251604/

Although its actual age continues to be disputed, some archaeologists believed that it came from the region of Tepe Sabz, Iran (the Mesopotamian area) circa 5500 to 5000 BC. One of nature's products, linen could be dyed quite easily, always retaining color when washed.

Ahhhhhh, so this was how the Acadians may have come into some of their more festive colored garments, yes?

Knowing that the finished product would only get softer and finer the more it was washed, while still retaining both its strength and durability, Madeleine was most eager to begin weaving small items like handkerchiefs.

Mother Pêche would be able to barter some for the things she needed.

Madeleine was more than happy to be able to give back to Mother Pêche in this way.

She was also instructed to make some items for herself, items that she would be able to use in the future.

Learning how to make braided rugs from worn clothing was superbly easy. One began by cutting the material into long strips. It soon became apparent to Madeleine that the longer the strips, the larger the finished rug.

You started by tying three strips together. You had to have someone hold the tied end for you. Either that or you would find something heavy to place on the tied end.

As soon as you had braided enough length to prevent the tied end from twisting unnecessarily, you could remove the heavy object or release the helper.

Continuing to braid all lengths in the same fashion, you then had to sew the loose ends together. Then you would begin to coil the braid carefully on the wooden table, starting from the center and working your way outward.

For a circular rug, Madeleine learned that she needed to coil the braids in a circle, starting with a very small coil.

For an oval shape, she was instructed to lay one foot of braided strips along the length of the large wooden table.

Holding the strip down firmly, she worked to begin the coil around the one-foot braid.

As soon as she had decided on the shape for her rug, she had to start sewing the rows of coil to each other, making sure to keep all of the stitches on the top side of the rug. It was in the experimenting with possible shapes that Madeleine also made several large pot holders as well.

Madeleine soon discovered that Mother Pêche was also eager to demonstrate the art of embroidery, something to which her young charge took an immediate liking.

It was not long before she was creating the most beautiful table runners, placemats and handkerchiefs in all of Grand Pré.

Chapter 8

Both Madeleine and Mother Pêche had kept themselves busy the long winter months. Michel was a daily visitor still. He and Madeleine had become close, often chatting about life and its purpose.

Mother Pêche knew that all was unfolding as had been written, for they were soon to fall deeply in love. In her enterprising to provide them with quality time, she would often retreat to the loft for her daily meditations.

While this time was respected, Madeleine had to remember that courtship in 1755 was vastly different from that of 2005. Michel was forever amazed, all in a good way of course, that he and Madeleine were able to converse about metaphysical topics, much like his conversations with Mother Pêche.

There was no other soul in the village who was interested in things of an unexplainable and synchronistic nature. He knew that he had found his soul mate.

They now laughed about their first awkward moment, one morning during breakfast when both had reached for the same piece of bread, only to wind up holding hands.

At that time, Madeleine had been with Mother Pêche for a little over three months. Both ended up with flushed faces as a result of the unexpected contact.

Madeleine quickly lowered her eyes to her plate, positioning her hands in her lap, unconsciously twisting the folds of her dress.

Michel began to clear his throat.

Mother Pêche, unable to contain herself, immediately broke into peals of laughter. When she laughed her strange, cackle-like laugh, there was no holding onto your own. Within seconds, all were laughing hysterically.

Mother Pêche could do naught but wipe the tears from her eyes.

"You, two, have been walking around each other as if on egg shells. I was so wondering when something like this was going to happen. Good. We are finally over this first hurdle."

After that morning, following mandatory chores, Madeleine and Michel had begun to take walks around the property. At first they walked closely, shoulder to shoulder; within several weeks they were holding hands.

During the winter months, when they were holed up inside due to inclement weather, they would often sit, talking, before the fire, with their arms wrapped around each other. Time stood still during these special moments.

Over the course of nine years, Michel had become quite adept at balancing his time between Mother Pêche and his own family. Despite the long work hours, Michel looked forward to the time he was given to reflect upon life when he was with Mother Pêche. Food for the soul, this was what provided him with the necessary sustenance to return to his family homestead, ready to engage in the work requested, and expected, of him.

Well pleased with the skills that Mother Pêche had shared with her, Madeleine was quite eager to present Michel with a very special gift, a handkerchief embroidered with their names and intertwined within hearts.

The moment she gifted him with such, he clasped her to his heart, brushing his lips across her forehead with such incredible tenderness that tears, filling her eyes, overflowed down her cheeks.

Michel lovingly wiped her tears away with the handkerchief. Then he kissed her. It was the sweetest, most loving, kiss that Madeleine had ever experienced.

This was the moment that would remain forever etched on her soul, for it was a few moments later that Michel asked her to marry him.

Madeleine was filled with a sense of completeness.

She knew that her life had come full circle for this particular moment in time. She also knew that there would be other such moments throughout their life together.

Their betrothal was now official.

Michel had not shown interest in any other female in the village. Both Honoré and Geneviève were pleased with Michel's choice, welcoming Madeleine into the family fold. With a wedding date set for August 16, 1755, Madeleine's upcoming twenty-seventh birthday, such gave the betrothed couple six months to begin accruing the items that would be needed for their own home.

The villagers were so enthralled with the weaving and embroidery talents of this wee slip of a girl, that it was not long before every homestead in the village was a showcase to her finery. Indeed, it was this very talent that would allow Michel to barter for items of necessity, at times acquired through Louisbourg, at others from New England.

Mother Pêche had gifted them with a significant piece of property, adjacent to hers, but closer to the Gaspereau River. In the end, it was decided that Madeleine and Michel would take up residence with Madame until their own home was built and ready for them.

It was not long before the spring of 1755 had arrived. With everyone involved in the tilling of the soil and the planting of the gardens, there were very few moments to spare.

Knowing that she and Michel would soon be married filled her every waking moment.

Such were joyful thoughts, and yet she sensed that Mother Pêche was very worried about something of significant importance.

Ever since the British had established themselves at Halifax in 1749, thereby enabling them to substantially increase Britain's investment in Nova Scotia, she could easily sense that something was afoot.

She was also aware that many of the Mi'kmaq seemed to have regarded Britain's unilateral founding of Halifax a breach of the peace terms of 1725.

A delegation of ten Acadian Deputies, "Alexander Herbert, Annapolis; Joseph Dugad, Annapolis; Claude LeBlanc, Grand Pré; Jean Melançon, River Canard; Baptiste Gaillard, Piziquid; Pierre Doucet, Chignecto; François Bourg, Chignecto; and Alexander Brossart, Chipoudie" [31] had journeyed to Halifax, arriving on July 29, 1749, the purpose of their command being to inform the English military, under Colonel Edward Cornwallis, who among the people (that each represented) was willing to sign the oath that had been demanded of them.

In addition to Cornwallis, this military team also consisted of Colonel Peregrine Thomas Hopson, Colonel Jean Paul Mascarene, Lieutenant Colonel John Horseman, and Major Charles Lawrence.

In keeping with the recorded minutes was written "[your people must] take the Oath of Allegiance as offered them, for His Majesty would allow none to possess lands in His territory whose allegiance and assistance in case of need

---

[31] Landry, Peter. (2008). *History of Nova Scotia: Book 1, Part 6, Chapter 6: The Deportation of the Acadians* accessed on November 16, 2008 at www.blupete.com/Hist/NovaScotiaBk1/Part6/Ch06.htm

could not be depended upon. And that such as should behave as true subjects ought to do will be supported and encouraged and protected equally with the rest of His Majesty's subjects." [32]

The Deputies were then dispatched to their communities with the message to all that they had until October 26, 1749, to sign this oath.

While grateful for everything that the British had done for them, the Acadian people felt that signing an unconditional oath, as dictated, would open them up to being attacked by the Mi'kmaq peoples that they had long befriended.

The Acadians were a peaceable people, a neutral people. It was for this very reason that they were "resolved *not* to take the oath unless they were exempted from taking up arms. Indeed, they explained, they had already taken such an oath, years ago, when Richard Phillips was governor, and it was

---

[32] Landry, Peter. (2008). *History of Nova Scotia: Book 1, Part 6, Chapter 6: The Deportation of the Acadians* accessed on November 16, 2008 at www.blupete.com/Hist/NovaScotiaBk1/Part6/Ch06.htm

understood by those that signed that they and their heirs were bound by it." [33]

In keeping, it was what they shared next that astonished Cornwallis.

"If your Excellency is not disposed to grant us what we take the liberty of asking, we are resolved, every one of us, to leave the country." [34]

Might these very words have been remembered by Major Charles Lawrence when he was officially sworn in as Lieutenant Governor of Nova Scotia on October 21, 1754?

Mother Pêche had managed to push these thoughts from her mind, quite successfully at that, until July 1755, when all arms in the possession of the Acadians had been confiscated; it was clear to see that a storm had been brewing over the refusal of Acadians to sign the oath of allegiance to the king

---

[33] Landry, Peter. (2008). *History of Nova Scotia: Book 1, Part 6, Chapter 6: The Deportation of the Acadians* accessed on November 16, 2008 at www.blupete.com/Hist/NovaScotiaBk1/Part6/Ch06.htm
[34] Ibid.

of England. A few Acadians, fearing the worst, agreed to sign the oath unconditionally. Their request was refused.

Since the re-establishment of the French settlers at Port Royal in 1635, Grand Pré had grown to become the largest of all the Acadian settlements. Madeleine, quite aware of her maternal Acadian history, was now remembering and identifying with the soon-to-be deported peoples of these fertile and majestic lands. Mind you, she was unable to remember the exact dates.

With the marriage date set, and a mere six weeks away, Madeleine was beginning to panic.

"I am feeling so on edge because these kind hearted people have absolutely no idea what lies in store for them. I have no idea what lies in store for me. What are we to do?"

"Do not despair, dear one, for I have the beginnings of a plan. Do you remember the root cellar hiding place below the foundation of this homestead?"

"Oh, my goodness, it's the tunnel, isn't it?"

"As you have been able to surmise, the tunnel below is not your typical tunnel. You are the very first soul that I am about to share this with. Do you remember wondering about how I had come to be here, some nine years previous?"

"The tunnel is linked to some quantum travel mechanism, isn't it?" Madeleine began clapping her hands with glee. "And this is how Michel and I shall make our way back to the twenty-first century, correct?"

"That is indeed so, dearest Madeleine. There appears to be some sort of energy vortex associated with this tunnel. Perhaps this was also known to the previous inhabitant, the healer of the village. I cannot even say how it is that I first chanced across this energy vortex, except to say that I was living in La Rochelle, France, at the time, as Jacques de Molay."

Madeleine was shocked.

"How can it be, then, that you leave one place as a male and travel to another place as a female? That is what I cannot understand. This means that you have to return to your time, a time whereby you shall eventually be burned alive on an island in the Seine river, in front of the Cathedral Notre Dame de Paris.

"Why would you even be wanting to go back? Would it not be better for you to remain here, as bad and as horrific as the deportation is going to be?"

Mother Pêche just answered with a sad, tired smile.

"My life, as is also the case with yours, has been put on hold. I have to return, dear one, simply to fulfill my duty and responsibility to my Templar brethren, but enough about me. Let us think about how we are going to broach this incredible topic with Michel."

Chapter 9

Morning came too soon, and still Mother Pêche and Madeleine were no further ahead and as perplexed as ever. How were they to even begin to discuss this with Michel?

This was not going to be an easy task. How did one explain the future to someone who was not even aware that they have had a past, let alone a prospective future?

"Perhaps we need to take Michel back to the time of the Mayan civilization, talking about the fact that they were avid stargazers, "renowned for their architectural, artistic, mathematical and scientific achievements," [35] having left us with "a series of super-human sized stone monuments and pyramids with precise calendrical computations." [36] What do you think, dearest Madeleine?"

---

[35] 13 Moons of Peace. (2005). *The Mayan Prophecy of 2012* accessed on November 16, 2008 at www.13moon.com/prophecy%20page.htm
[36] Ibid.

Madeleine was quick to warm up to the subject. "With their extensive knowledge about astrology, they had developed calendars based on logic, science and nature, knowing that time was a qualitative essence.

"It was not until the advent of the Gregorian Calendar that we began to see time as something outside of ourselves. This is why we are so hung up on time, especially in the twenty-first century. It is in seeing time as "something linear, containable, and separate from the organic flowing process of life" [37] that we have created so much unnecessary limitation."

Mother Pêche began to smile, allowing Madeleine to continue.

"Just taking stock of the people and their lives here has given me time to rethink the way that I want to live my life, especially upon my return. In keeping with our spiritual natures, we have forgotten that we, too, are time for it is known that the "synchronic order of natural time governs the

---

[37] 13 Moons of Peace. (2005). *The Mayan Prophecy of 2012* accessed on November 16, 2008 at www.13moon.com/prophecy%20page.htm

unfolding of our lives. Time's cycles are found within our bodies and within Nature's daily rhythms and cyclic seasons." [38] We have forgotten this, thinking that time is money, thinking that time is the clock, thinking that time is the relentless progression of work weeks and weekends.

"Quite true, Madeleine, quite true. You are giving me much to ponder and reflect upon."

"What we have also failed to remember is that "time is the ever-changing, unfolding Now as it synchronistically coordinates the whole living universe" [39] of which we are a significant part."

Mother Pêche nodded in agreement.

"We must also remember, my good Mother, that the Native American traditions, including those of the Lakota, Cherokee and Hopi, indicate that my time in history is the

---

[38] 13 Moons of Peace. (2005). *The Mayan Prophecy of 2012* accessed on November 16, 2008 at www.13moon.com/prophecy%20page.htm
[39] Ibid.

time of their prophecies, the close of a grand cycle leading to the birth of a new world, a sixth world of consciousness."

"Indeed, Madeleine, the Mayan culture was a truly amazing one. Their calendar, an ancient system of time keeping, was predicted to find completion in the year 2012 AD, which is that of your time, dear one; hence, the prophecies of the aboriginal peoples of whom you speak."

"This is so, my Mother. Their system of time keeping dates back some 18,000 years ago, a fact that is beyond current human understanding, at least to the multitude. Most are completely astounded that this ancient calendar was able to predict that my time in history would be the one they deemed the lifetime for change. Is this why Michel and I have to go back? Are we to be part of this change in the collective consciousness of the planet?"

Mother Pêche smiled a most knowing smile. "*Now* you are beginning to both understand and accept your role in this drama, little one. You have done well to piece it all together. Such is the purpose of this grand shift for all life forms, including Mother Earth herself.

"In order to begin to express life through a much higher frequency, a Christed energy if you will, there must be healing and balance. In having said this, "each individual now living upon the Earth is an *integral* part of The Shift process, playing the vital role of midwife in the birth of a new era of human perception and awareness." [40]

In addition, "the relationship between Earth, the planetary magnetic fields, and cellular function of the body is a key component to the understanding of the consciousness evolution and the process of The Shift." [41]

Madeleine gave a most unladylike snort.

"I do not think that I am going to readily grasp what you are about to disclose, for I have neither a keen interest, nor understanding, in either mathematics or science. In my final year of high school, I was unable to complete the academic math program, having to downgrade to a basic level. I almost didn't get into university as a result."

---

[40] Braden, Gregg. (1997). *Awakening to Zero Point: The Collective Initiation* (p. 12). Bellevue, WA: Radio Bookstore Press.
[41] Ibid, page 13.

"Then I shall do my utmost to assist you in grasping the rudimentary basics of what I am about to share. As well you know, the Earth is surrounded by its own magnetic field. It takes approximately 2,000 years for "the fields of magnetics to make one complete rotation around the surface of the Earth." [42] Over the course of this time span, the intensity of the Earth's magnetic fields have been dropping, more noticeably within your time. As "magnetics are a function of planetary rotations, a lessening in the intensity of magnetics would seem to indicate a lessening in the rate of the Earth's rotation" [43] as well."

"While I seem to be following you so far, I am not understanding the equated connection to the change in the consciousness of the planet."

Mother Pêche smiled before continuing. "It appears, then, that "the effects of global magnetics are not confirmed to individuals on a personal level. Variable planetary magnetics provide zones of experience where mass units of

---

[42] Braden, Gregg. (1997). *Awakening to Zero Point: The Collective Initiation* (p. 21). Bellevue, WA: Radio Bookstore Press.
[43] Ibid, p. 19.

consciousness are drawn to feel or work out some form of common experience. When an individual or group consciousness feels that an area no longer feels appropriate, or resonates with them, they are describing their body's sensors to those zones of magnetic density." [44]

Madeleine nodded, albeit slowly, a deeply contemplative look on her face, before Mother Pêche continued.

"The understanding of the nature of these fields is perhaps a vital key to understanding mass migrations of large populations, human and animal alike, as well as the unexplained settling of ancient cultures in what may appear to be very unlikely locations for commerce or spiritual pursuits." [45]

"I remember watching a documentary about Chaco Canyon in northwestern New Mexico. It was featured on the History

---

[44] Braden, Gregg. (1997). *Awakening to Zero Point: The Collective Initiation* (pp. 19-20). Bellevue, WA: Radio Bookstore Press.
[45] Ibid, p. 20.

Channel. Might these zones of magnetic density have had something to do with that civilization?"

Mother Pêche smiled. "You see, you really do understand more than you give yourself credit for."

"Mind you, it is only because I have such a wonderfully patient and informative teacher."

"You are not without your own knowledge base, dearest. What needs to be remembered, Madeleine, is that "these lower values of magnetics are what provide the opportunity for change. Of course, the exact opposite holds true in areas of higher magnetic zones, whereby stagnation may be the result." Stagnation merely refers to the fact that one stops progressing, that one stops advancing. Individuals like us would feel the energies of such an area to be sluggish, to be dull. All in all, "these zones simply offer the opportunity for change." [46] How the opportunity is expressed becomes the choice of those experiencing the change."

---

[46] Braden, Gregg. (1997). *Awakening to Zero Point: The Collective Initiation* (p. 20). Bellevue, WA: Radio Bookstore Press.

"Let me see if I am understanding. You seem to be saying that we are poised on the threshold of a new paradigm of experience, one in which Michel and I have a significant role to play, and it is all due to the change in planetary magnetics?"

Madeleine still looked a wee bit unsure.

"That is *exactly* right, my sweet. You must also remember that the human form is both electrical as well as magnetic. At a time when planetary magnetics were relatively high, such ensured "that to manifest something in this world, we had to be very clear and really choose, or desire that which was being envisioned." [47] The planet, in your time, with considerably lessened magnetics, is now heading in a different direction."

"I think that I am still following you, my Mother."

Madeleine took several deep breaths before continuing.

---

[47] Braden, Gregg. (1997). *Awakening to Zero Point: The Collective Initiation* (p. 20). Bellevue, WA: Radio Bookstore Press.

"You have already shared that the magnetic fields of the Earth have been dropping over the course of these last 2,000 years. As a result, these lower magnetic fields are providing us with the very opportunity for change that we have been wanting, that we have been praying for.

"Not only that, but these lower magnetic fields mean that we are more rapidly able to manifest what we want in our lives, because it is in the thinking, feeling and expanding the emotion that we are our own creators."

It was now Mother Pêche's turn to clap her hands with glee. Beaming at Madeleine, she spoke further. "You have done so very well, my young and impressionable student. I am well pleased.

"Indeed, "it is in the space of resonance, attained simply from your patterns of *thought coupled with feeling*, that you may direct energy most efficiently, consciously and with intent. It is in this space that you become the creator of your experience and may impact the events of your world while regulating the response of your body to that world." [48] This is why it has become so important to carefully monitor your thoughts."

"This, then, is where I must *become* that which I desire more of in my life, isn't it? I must become the very experience that I most desire for myself and others – things like love, peace, forgiveness, nonjudgment and compassion."

"This might well be the very position that we have to take, Madeleine, thank you. I shall definitely give this further thought, but aside from that we shall let this day pass just as any other." She stretched and sighed. "Come to think of it, my sweet, you are both going to be busy harvesting vegetables. That will give me the time I need to organize my thoughts. Let us cease fretting for now. Nothing comes of constant worry, save stress and misery."

The next morning, July 29, 1755, was a brilliantly sunny and warm one.

---

[48] Braden, Gregg. (1997). *Awakening to Zero Point: The Collective Initiation* (p. 27). Bellevue, WA: Radio Bookstore Press.

Mother Pêche was exhausted from mulling the same pieces of the story over and over again. The remainder of the day passed well into the night.

Reflecting back on what she had shared with Madeleine, in keeping with the events at Montségur in 1244, several knights, possibly three, had scaled the mountain, escaping under the cover of total darkness, with the treasure of the Cathars, an important treasure of a tri-fold nature.

She had addressed the fact that Yeshua had two wives, an acceptable and encouraged position for a Jewish Rabbi of his time; first married to Miriam (of Bethany of the House of Saul) [49] as has clearly been delineated in the Bible, with a second marriage to Mirium (of the House of Æthiopia) known as Magdalene, [50] a fact that both the writers and compilers of the Bible have tried to further misconstrue by

---

[49] Montgomery, Hugh. (2006). *The God-Kings of Europe: The Descendants of Jesus Traced Through the Odonic and Davidic Dynasties* (p. 32). San Diego, CA: The Book Tree.
[50] Ibid.

taking the identities of both women and merging them into one being.

The Cathari treasure that had been secreted down the mountain of Montségur was [1] a direct female descendant of the Elchasai line, courtesy of Miriam of Bethany (Madeleine's line), [2] a direct female descendant connected with the Æthiopian line, courtesy of Mirium Magdalene (Michel's line), and [3] a copy of a book as written by Yeshua himself.

In keeping with Madeleine's claim to Yeshua, "the Elchasaites were an early Judaic-Christian sect who were also called *Mughtasilab* by al-Nadim and *Katharioi* (from which we get the name Cathar) in the Manicheaen work, *Kephalaia*," [51] proving that these ancestors of hers were the forerunners of the Cathars.

---

[51] Montgomery, Hugh. (2006). *The God-Kings of Europe: The Descendants of Jesus Traced Through the Odonic and Davidic Dynasties* (p. 34). San Diego, CA: The Book Tree.

As an added protective nature, it was this particular female descendant of Miriam of Bethany, of the Elchasai line, who had also married into the Sinclair family in Scotland.

Henceforth, *both* Michel (*dit Sophie*) and Madeleine were direct Grail descendants.

In addition, both were descendants sporting the *same birthmark*, another sign that they were *the ones* decreed to perpetuate the line, with their union bringing forth the notable Grail Child of the twenty-first century.

Aside from this mind reconfiguring, courtesy of Mother Pêche, Madeleine had no way of knowing that Yeshua's book had long been secreted across the waters to Nova Scotia, passed along to the aboriginal mother of the male child, born to Henry I Sinclair, for safekeeping. In turn, she had gifted her son with the valuable work.

It had since been passed in a direct line of descent, from father to son to son to son, meaning that a Mi'kmaq cousin to Madeleine was currently in receipt of this priceless and treasured tome.

Unbeknownst to Madeleine, Mother Pêche had already secured a meeting between cousins, but before it could come to pass, she also knew that she was going to have to disclose much more to Michel. There was simply no other way.

Several days later, Mother Pêche did just that.

Not wanting to bias him in any way, she asked that they travel to the old oak tree adjacent to the Gaspereau River, in order to break their fast. Given that this was also to become the homestead property of Madeleine and Michel following their marriage, Michel was sure to suspect nothing.

Such would also give Madeleine ample opportunity to become acclimatized to the fact that Michel was about to learn everything that she knew, including *where* she had come from.

While she was finding this to be rather disconcerting, she, too, knew that there was no other way.

With the date being August 1, 1755, Madeleine also knew that time was of the essence.

Chapter 10

"My dear Michel, we have engaged in many a metaphysical discourse these past nine years, have we not?"

"You are right, my good Mother, we have. Why do you ask?"

"I have something of considerable significance to share with you today. Long have I looked upon you as a dear son. I find that I have also come to look upon Madeleine as a daughter. What I am about to share concerns both of you. I want to deal with this topic appropriately and adequately, and yet I have no idea how much time I shall need in which to do so. Ergo, I shall do my very best."

Mother Pêche took several deep breaths before continuing.

"Long have you and I talked about the meaning of time, Michel. When asked to define time, every individual has their own answer. Outside of the rising and setting of the sun, signifying the beginning and ending of one's day, can time be measured? Indeed, time is observable, but can it be measured?

With a furrow across her brow, it was evident that Mother Pêche was still taking the time to organize her thoughts.

"How important is time? Better yet, are we dependent on time? On the flip side, is time dependent on anything? Does time operate independently or might there be other factors affiliated with time? If time does affect our reality, how does this happen? Is time real? Is time an illusion? Does time only flow in one direction?"

Michel looked at Mother Pêche with a knowing look.

"Never before have I been able to recall you taking the time to delve so deeply, and immediately at that, in any of our previous conversations. Knowing that you are about to share something profound, I trust that I am worthy enough to be graced with what you are about to divulge. If I may be truthful, I am feeling most on edge right now."

"As am I, my son, as am I. I shall do my best to proceed."

Mother Pêche made sure that she was completely comfortable before continuing. "In accordance with the religion of this community, time is seen to be linear, having a distinct beginning, referred to as the act of creation by God. What if time were not linear, but cyclical?"

Mother Pêche took a momentary pause. "The Mayan people, for example, were able to produce extremely accurate astronomical observations based on the fact that they believed time to be cyclical, meaning that time travels in circles."

"Ah, yes, the people who built remarkable pyramids and cities. I was always so intrigued with them from a mathematical and scientific point of view, being the master architects that they were, creating cities with complete drainage systems as well as amazingly comprehensive irrigation systems. While our dykes in no way can compare, they have been the answer to our situation."

Mother Pêche nodded in complete agreement.

"Knowing that the Mayan were located at a considerable distance from other advanced civilizations, like those found in Egypt, Greece and even Mesopotamia, their knowledge of time, astronomy and mathematics was truly astounding. For example, their calculation of the Earth's annual cycle was a great deal more accurate than any other such calculations that were in existence. By comparison to the Gregorian Calendar, of which you are familiar, the Mayan calculated one annual year to be 365.242036 days, just slightly longer than our 365 days."

"One certainly has to take the time to admire and respect a culture that existed well in advance of us here in 1755."

"You are quite right, Michel. Truth be told, we can learn much from those who have come and gone before us if we but take the time to do so. Too many times, however, we have believed ourselves to be infallible, have we not?"

Michel smiled in acknowledgment.

Mother Pêche continued, as per her cue.

"What truly makes all of this so very fascinating is the fact that the Mayans developed their long count calendar in 3114 BC. It was at this same time that the earliest stages of Stonehenge were being astronomically aligned and set in place.

"Following the unification of Upper and Lower Egypt, it was in north Africa, during this same time, that the first Dynastic period began. Hieroglyphs, a combination of logoglyphs and alphabetic elements, emerged there. Likewise, it was in Mesopotamia that cuneiform script, the earliest known writing script in the world, was developed.

"The Hindu religion was being formed in India. A Neolithic settlement was built at Skara Brae in the Orkney Islands. The New Stone Age people of Ireland built Newgrange, a solar oriented passage tomb.

"Individually, all of these events would be considered a cultural revolution. Collectively, however, it marked the beginning of a paradigm shift in consciousness, for such was a quantum leap in the evolution of mankind."

Mother Pêche was quick to offer Michel a smile. "Madeleine would be pleased with my fine lead into the topic of what is referred to as a paradigm shift, for I, myself, am quite amazed at how easily this is coming about."

"What do you mean by this word, by this *paradigm*?"

"The word paradigm refers to a conceptual framework, a belief system, an overall prospective, through which we see and interpret the world. As such, one's paradigm determines what they are able to see, how they think and what they do. For example, how one views the world, by way of a spiritual tradition, is part of the individual paradigm to which they adhere.

"That having been said, paradigms are relative, subjective and personal. We assume that the way we see things is the way they really are. Our paradigms become perceptible to us only when we encounter one that differs from our own."

Michel nodded his head in complete understanding.

"As has been the case since my meeting you nine years ago.

"You are telling me, my good Mother, that as a result of our meeting, our verbal exchange, our connecting with each other, that my paradigm has shifted."

"This is exactly so, my Michel. Now comes the tricky part, the asking of pertinent questions that tell us much about our own paradigms.

"There are those who choose to see the world as a battlefield with good forces pitting against evil; others see the world as a classroom where we come to learn and are put through a multitude of tests. We can also choose to see the world as a trap, whereby we attempt to disentangle ourselves in order to ascend to a higher plane of tranquility; so, too, can one choose to see the world as a partner, attempting to commune more with nature in an effort to become more fully human. Better yet, we can choose to see the world as self, an interconnected whole with each playing an important role in the overall script of life. These are the types of questions that one must continue to ponder."

Michel appeared to be quite excited. "I think that I am actually getting this!"

With furrowed brow, he deliberated for a few moments, in an effort to organize his thoughts. "I need to ask myself questions like, what belief system do I operate from and how are these paradigms serving me in this life?

"You are clearly saying, my good Mother, that one way to know yourself, or at least understand where you are now, is by asking yourself questions of great importance. What do I value? What are my needs? What are my feelings? What matters to me? How do I fit into the grand scheme called life? How do I know what I know? What is truth?"

Mother Pêche was overwhelmed with relief that Michel was grasping so much. "Yes, the more you know about who you are, the easier it is to respond (as opposed to react) to life. Everything we do, and say, is the expression of our beliefs about the world. Finding and identifying those underlying beliefs can lead to both insight and understanding.

"As one would also expect, paradigms shift when we change from one way of thinking to another way of thinking. It can be compared to a revolution, a transformation, a sort of metamorphosis, if you will. However, it is not simply something that just happens out of the blue and on its own; rather, it is driven by agents of change. For the greater multitude, as well you know, change is difficult."

Mother Pêche sighed deeply. "You are now wanting to know how it is that paradigms shift, correct?"

Michel nodded in a solemn and serious manner before Mother Pêche delved further.

"World views emerge to solve problems. For an emerging new world view to take hold, the majority have to fully understand, aside from abstract intellect, that the current way of thinking is no longer adequate to solve the problems that they are being faced with.

"It is not enough to be passionate about the change that is needed, nor is it satisfactory to suppress the voices of those in disagreement. Even here, in 1755, we are being challenged to combine rational and nonrational (faith, intuition, spiritual insight, nature, body-based wisdom) ways of thinking. Having said this, a new world view is in the process of arriving."

"Truly, I am in awe, my good Mother. While we have been discussing much, it feels like there is so much more to come."

"Do you remember, Michel, when we first spoke about the concept of reincarnation?"

Michel smiled. "I rather enjoyed learning that upon one's physical death the soul leaves the body, only to be reintroduced to another physical body. While I cannot prove that reincarnation exists, I fail to see how the Creator would give me but one chance at life, let alone one chance at having a lifetime with Madeleine. We have so much in common that it feels as if I have known her forever."

"Quite right, Michel. Do you also remember my sharing that in the living of these many lives, that we have lived both as male as well as female?"

Michel nodded in the affirmative.

"Well, my dearest Michel, what I am about to share next will elicit a reaction from you, of that I am sure. How you choose to react will be in keeping with the paradigm to which you adhere.

"Not only are there past lives, but there are future lives as well. So, too, are there parallel lives, a concept that I, myself, am still struggling with.

"You see, I came to you in 1746 from the time period of 1305, propelled 441 years into the future. At that time, I was a male and living in France. While I am unsure as to how I came to be here as a female, it may well be a case of what I have called a parallel life. While very different from one's current life, it has been said that parallel lives may actually be complementary in nature. Perhaps this is why I am here, before you, in the female form.

"Madeleine has come to your time from the future, from the year 2005, a period of exactly 700 years from 1305, and yet we are all here together. She is here because her destiny has been intertwined with yours, meaning that you are both meant to return to the twenty-first century. Yours is a shared destiny that has much to do with bloodlines and the true teachings of the one known as Yeshua."

While Michel was a tad mesmerized after Mother Pêche had finished, he was not nearly as troubled as she had expected him to be.

Having been able to take her time discussing each piece of the ever-growing puzzle, she was pleased. Michel was certainly quick with the questions each time he was not following. Likewise for the acknowledging comments as he was understanding.

"So you see, Michel, you and Madeleine have been linked long before you came into this particular incarnation. In respecting each other, you have also come to care deeply for each other, which is as it should be. I shant worry, knowing that the two of you are together, as has long since been decreed by the stars." Mother Pêche stopped, taking the time to observe Michel.

"I have often wondered, my good Mother, how it is that you have come by so much knowledge, not of your time."

Mother Pêche gave a solemn, yet slight, nod of the head.

"As a Templar brother with many friends in the Arabic world, there were many sacred texts that I came to discover during my time in Outremer. These texts had recorded an oral history long forgotten by those living in the western world.

"As a Templar brother of notable leverage, I was also privy to much that was discovered at Solomon's Temple, courtesy of a series of vertical tunnels ascending to the site of the Al Aqsa Mosque and then spreading out to the Dome of the Rock. Of course, this was information that we had to keep quiet for reasons of our own accord.

"I have also been privy to information in accordance with my psychic abilities; hence, my knowledge in reference to both past as well as future."

"Thank you for sharing this, my good Mother. Do you mind if I take a walk for a few minutes? This is much to take in."

"You do what you need to do, Michel. I shall take the time to meditate further, here with my ancient friend, the old oak tree. We can continue this conversation upon your return."

Ten minutes later, Michel returned to the old oak tree. Mother Pêche, true to her word, had been meditating, eyes closed with a soft smile of deep contentment on her face. Giving him time to resettle, she continued to reflect in silence.

"You look very happy, Mother Pêche."

"That is because I have been able to share much with you this fine morning.

"Truly, I was feeling so burdened at not being able to share my knowledge, and yet there is still so much more."

"Of that, I am certain." Michel paused before continuing. "If Madeleine is from my future, and I am supposed to return with her, how do you propose that we do so? I just cannot fathom how this can be."

"I, too, was of this same understanding until it happened to me. Then it happened to Madeleine. Now you are able to see why I could not share this with you upon my arrival, why I could not share this with the villagers.

"They know that Madeleine, my godchild, has come to spend time with me. Given her family affiliation with the Templar Knights, I can say that this is indeed true.

"There is a tunnel that I need to show you within the next few days, a tunnel hidden within the very foundation of my homestead. It was courtesy of this tunnel that I came to be here with you. It may also have been through this same tunnel that the former inhabitant, the healer of the village, disappeared, but, of course, I am only surmising."

"Is Madeleine aware of this tunnel?"

"Yes, she is quite aware, for it is in the very root cellar adjacent to the tunnel itself that we have hidden her personal belongings, given that all are from the future."

As always, Michel was very cognizant of the time. "Perhaps this is enough for one day, my good Mother. We should probably be getting back."

"Yes, you are quite right. Over the course of the next few days, I shall take the time to further disclose my thoughts about the tunnel with both of you."

"Had you shared this with me when you first arrived, close to ten years ago, I would have thought that maybe you were losing your mind. After all, how can one leave one's life as a male, arriving in another as a female, only to return to said time as the aforementioned male? I find that I am unable to grasp this concept."

"Truth be told, my son, I do not totally understand it myself. I can only tell you from whence I directly came, knowing full well that I have to return after my work here has been fulfilled."

"And when will that be?"

"I feel that it will be very soon, Michel. Assuredly, before the winter has come over this beautiful land. It is now time to return to Madeleine. I have to arrange for her to meet a Mi'kmaq cousin, the next phase of this most important assignment."

Riding back to the homestead in companionable silence, both had much to contemplate.

Madeleine was more than happy, and relieved, to greet them both. She and Michel shared a few intimate words before he was off to the village.

"Michel appears to have taken the news well. You must be so comforted, my good Mother. I know that I surely am."

Madeleine let out a long, pent-up sigh. "While it felt awful not being able to share this knowledge with him, it felt even worse knowing that I was from the future, doing my best to pretend to fit in."

"Yes, I quite understand how it feels to be burdened with heavy secrets, my child. I find that I am now quite tired, so I think that I shall rest for a wee bit."

"I, too, have been fretting all morning. I think that I shall also take the time to rest."

Together they entered the house, both quickly drifting off into a deep and much needed sleep.

Chapter 11

The very next morning, August 2, 1755, Madeleine was ecstatic to learn that Mother Pêche had made contact with a Mi'kmaq Sinclair cousin. Using the terminology of the twenty-first century, this was going to be a meeting of monumental and historic proportions.

Living a considerable distance from the village, Mother Pêche knew that Madeleine and Gabriel would find privacy on the property.

Arriving several days later, Madeleine was instantly struck by the raw beauty of her cousin. Long, straight, blue black hair, plaited into a single braid, falling down the middle of his back, he stood tall.

Proud of his dual ancestry, he exuded strength, fortitude and acceptance. It was tuning into these feelings that Madeleine was finally able to relax. Much to her astonishment, she responded by bursting into tears, feverishly trying to wipe them away as fast as they were coming.

146

Gabriel responded by enfolding Madeleine in his arms, allowing her to work through her seesaw emotions.

"I am so sorry, Gabriel. I didn't mean to cry all over you. I have no idea why I've reacted this way."

"You are missing family, 'tis all, ma petite. We are family, although you come from a time far ahead of my own."

"You are most wise, cousin. I feel that I am here to learn a great deal from you."

"If I may add to that, in retrospect, we are here to learn from each other."

It was easy to read the wisdom in Gabriel's eyes. They looked at each other in silence for a moment. Suddenly, Gabriel's face was wreathed in a smile. All Madeleine could do was respond in kind.

"My good Mother Pêche has told me that you know of my heritage; that I, like you, am a direct descendant of Henry I Sinclair. While there are some, in your time, who would dispute such, it is what it is."

"And just what is it that you think individuals in my time would dispute?"

"First and foremost, the very fact that Henry Sinclair came to the New World, well before Christopher Columbus. Secondly, the very fact that I am standing before you now, a direct DNA cousin to you, a citizen of the twenty-first century."

"You know, I cannot emphasize enough that the history they teach in school pales dramatically in comparison to being here, to actually living it. While there will always be biases, it is hard to know who to believe, what to believe."

"Simply trust your heart, ma petite. If you trust and live by your heart, you will never be steered wrong."

"I am sure that you grew up in the tradition of the passing down of many stories, Gabriel. Always wondering why I was born with a birthmark that looked so bizarre, the history of my family was not shared with me.

"I truly had no idea what my birthmark was supposed to represent until I started delving into topics like the Knights Templar. That is when I knew that it was a Templar cross configuration.

"I became convinced that I was the only person to have such a marking, and then I was told that Michel also bears the same. Truly, I am still unsure what to make of all this."

"Surely, Madeleine, if you have delved into the Knights Templar, then you have also some degree of familiarity with the Merovingians, yes?"

Madeleine nodded before sharing what she knew.

"Known as the Long Haired Kings, they were reputed to have had magical powers of some kind that were actually attributed to their long hair.

"This dynasty gets its name from Mérovée. It is said that Mérovée was supposedly conceived when his mother, the wife of the king, encountered a Quinotaur (a sea monster that has the ability to change shape) while swimming.

"I prefer to think along the lines of a foreign conqueror, coming from the sea, taking the dead king's wife (already pregnant) as his own (thereby impregnating her once again) in order to legitimize his claim."

Gabriel smiled, waiting patiently, for Madeleine to continue.

"They were a Frankish tribe, able to establish a lasting realm that today covers part of France and Germany. In essence, the Merovingians [52] gave rise to the Carolingians, [53] the first ruler being King Charles I, known as Charlemagne. I am of the understanding that our Sinclair line takes us directly back to him.

"While the Merovingians claimed to be descended from Troy, the Tribe of Benjamin, and Arcadia, I have no idea if this can actually be proven. I have also read that they may have descended from a long line of pharaohs in ancient

---

[52] Stephan, Ed. (1999). *The Merovingian Kings* accessed on November 15, 2008 at www.edstephan.org/Rulers/merovingian.html

[53] Stephan, Ed. (1999). *House of Pepin: Dynasty of Charlemagne* accessed on November 15, 2008 at www.edstephan.org/Rulers/charlemagne.html

Egypt, including Rameses II, who was considered to be the greatest pharaoh of all.

"It was Clovis I who established his capital at Paris. It is he who has been accredited, historically, with the beginning of the Merovingian aristocracy. In fact, most of the European monarchs from the Middle Ages have been descendants of Merovingian lineage. While the Merovingians reigned, they did not rule. Instead, they chose to leave the secular governing function to chancellors who were known as the Mayors of the Palace. It was one of these Mayors, Pépin the Fat, who, in fact, founded the dynasty that came to supplant them; the Carolingians.

"Whether or not they were occult adepts may never be known, but the discovery in 1653 of a Merovingian tomb in Tournai led to a ring with an inscription CHILDERICI REGIS (meaning *of Childeric the King*), the piece that identified the tomb as belonging to King Childeric I, father of Clovis I.

"The tomb treasure and regalia were what one would expect to find in a royal tomb. Most interestingly, there were numerous pieces of gold, cloisonnéed with garnets, which also included 300 miniature bees.

"I remember being so intrigued by the bees in the tomb that I conducted several Internet searches, discovering that the bee was viewed as a sign of industry, creativity, wealth, diligence and eloquence, with the ancient Egyptians using it as a symbol to represent regal power. In this case, they were considered to be the oldest emblems of the sovereigns of France. It was guessed that these bees could have decorated a royal mantle, thereafter becoming the precursor [54] to the French fleurs-de-lys.

"They also found items that many have linked with magic and divination – a severed horse's head, a bull's head made of gold, and a crystal ball, which could very easily explain why they were also known as The Sorcerer Kings.

----

[54] Gough, Andrew. (2006). Arcadia. *The Bee: Part 3 – Beegotten* article accessed on November 15, 2008 at http://andrewgough.co.uk/articles_bee3/

"In addition, it is reputed that they could allegedly heal others by the laying on of hands. This might be very similar to what they refer to as Reiki in my time.

"I also read that they were supposed to have had a specific birthmark that was always situated between their shoulder blades. I am beginning to surmise that perhaps it was most similar to my own, which leads me into a totally different realm altogether.

"They say that people carry birthmarks, as well as all marks of violence from a previous life, into the next, which could well be the physical proof that reincarnation and biology actually intersect in this way.

"Having no past life memories, however, I have no way of explaining to you how it is that both Michel and myself carry the same birthmark; that about sums up what I can tell you about the Merovingians."

Gabriel smiled. "Your knowledge most impressive, ma petite. Do you know of the connection that exists between our direct ancestor, Henry Sinclair, and the Merovingians?"

"While I know that Henry Sinclair was the 1st Earl of Orkney, the Baron of Roslin and Lord of Shetland, later becoming the grandfather of William Sinclair, the builder of the Rosslyn Chapel, I am unaware of the direct connection."

Madeleine eagerly awaited the real history lesson that was about to unfold

"Henry Sinclair was also the grandmaster of the Scottish Freemasons. Interestingly enough, the first documented Masonic lodge meeting in North America took place at the Sinclair Inn, here in Annapolis Royal in 1738, a mere seventeen years ago. When you return to your time, you will find that this building still stands, having been deemed a National Historic Site.

"Another interesting connection refers to another known fact, one that you have already alluded to. As you know, there has existed much speculation surrounding why New Scotland later became known as Acadie, or Acadia (said to be a corruption of Arcadie or Arcadian). Those who believe the bloodline of Christ passed through the Merovingian kings will recall that Arcadia, Greece, was the first place to which Christ's descendants were alleged to have emigrated after leaving Judea before moving on to France. [55]

"In fact, there is a *direct* connection between the heirs of Yeshua, the Merovingians, the Cathars, and Rhedae, or Rennes-le-Château as it is known in your time. The Merovingians claim descent from Yeshua. The Cathars claim descent from Yeshua and both wives, of whom Mother Pêche has already spoken.

"The Knights Templar were deemed the protectors, the guardians, of the Blood Royal or Holy Grail. The Knights Templar were also affiliated with the Cathars. Henry Sinclair was a known patron of the Templar Knights, and, quite possibly, was a Templar Knight himself. In addition, the families who founded the Knights Templar were part of the same group of descendants known as the *Desposyni*."

---

[55] Burden, George. (2008). Oak Island Treasure. *Treasure in Nova Scotia?* Article accessed on December 7, 2008 at http://www.oakislandtreasure.co.uk/content/view/115/2/ Article accessed on March 28, 2017 at https://lifeasahuman.com/2010/travel-adventure/adventure/treasure-in-nova-scotia/

"You know, Gabriel, I can also remember learning about a document called the *Chinon Parchment* that surfaced in 2001. It was said to have been retrieved from the Vatican Secret Archives, proving to be a record of the trial of the Templars.

"Accordingly, Pope Clement V absolved them of all heresies in 1308, formally disbanding the order in 1312. If this is true, then why was Jacques de Molay arrested in 1307 and burnt at the stake in 1314? I know that Mother Pêche has access to this information, and I like it not. What can I do?"

"You can do nothing, ma petite, save allow her to live out the choices that have already been made."

"While I know there is much truth in your words, I cannot help the fact that I keep thinking about all of the forgeries instigated by the Catholic church over the years, like the Donation of Constantine. This was the formal edict that enabled the Carolingian family to supplant the royal Merovingian line. Well into the twelfth century, it was still being used by medieval popes to bolster their territorial and secular power. For the most part, it was widely accepted as authentic, at least until 1453."

"Thank you for bringing me to my next topic. As well you know, dearest Madeleine, the Cathars were a medieval sect who sought to achieve great spiritual purity. Believing in dualism, they acknowledged that both the light (God) and the dark (Devil) resided within every individual. It was at the beginning of the thirteenth century that "an army of northern knights descended on the Languedoc to stamp out the Cathar or Albigensian heresy" [56] and claim the rich spoils of the region for themselves."

"Yes, it was during the atrocities of this time that Rennes-le-Château was captured and transferred from hand to hand as a fief for some considerable time thereafter. [57] I can also remember reading that the village of Rennes-le-Château, located in southwestern France, had once been known as Rhedae, just as you have shared, Gabriel. It may have been the northern capital of the empire ruled by the Visigoths.

---

[56] Baigent, Michael, Leigh, Richard and Lincoln, Henry. (2004). *Holy Blood, Holy Grail* (p. 33). New York, NY: Delacorte Press.
[57] Ibid.

Many have surmised that Rhedae was a military stronghold of that time."

Gabriel nodded, encouraging Madeleine to continue.

"While I can see what you are saying, Gabriel, I am still not sure where this is going and how it connects or even why it connects."

"In their plan to both attain and remain in power, the Roman church knew what they were about, beginning first with the Merovingians. Thereafter, anyone and anything that stood in their way was either annihilated or destroyed. Many times, such also meant complete denigration of the truth."

They sat in companionable silence a moment before Gabriel stood up to remove something from his backpack. It was first wrapped in leather, followed by linen.

Upon realizing the gift of being granted the privilege to view such a special codex, Madeleine was humbled. Not wanting to delve amongst its pages, she quickly handed it back to Gabriel.

"This is the gift left behind by my ancestor, Henry Sinclair. We have long known that there would come a time when this volume would be passed to another of the Sinclair line.

"I have been instructed to present you with this special book, written in the Aramaic language of Yeshua's time. It is you, ma petite, who is to take it back to the twenty-first century, the time of the collective paradigm shift."

Madeleine sat still, tears streaming down her face, as Gabriel continued.

"There you will find a way to have its authenticity verified and validated for the world and its people. I also have a second volume, one written in Latin."

Gabriel lovingly handed the second tome to Madeleine.

"Mother Pêche has already completed the translation from Latin into French. From there, it can easily be translated into English as well as countless other languages; hence, the message of Yeshua will be able to reach one and all. This is but part of the mission that you have been entrusted with."

Madeleine felt the power of Gabriel's words. Indeed, she had a major role to play in bringing these volumes forth to the citizens of the world; more specifically, to the citizens of the twenty-first century.

At a deep instinctual level, Madeleine also knew that she and Michel were to live, and demonstrate, the very truths contained within, thereby becoming living examples to others.

"I have always been fascinated with the spiritual beliefs and practices of indigenous peoples. Might you be able to share something about your beliefs, dearest Gabriel?"

"It would be an honor to do so, ma petite.

"Traditional Mi'kmaq spirituality is animistic, meaning that we both "recognize and acknowledge the living spirit within all things. As one would expect, this encompasses the entire animal kingdom, but we also acknowledge the spirit within plants, and within the rocks and waters of our world. We also do not 'worship' these things. Instead, we recognize that their spirits and our own are akin to each other, and we treat these spirits with the same respect for ourselves. *Msit No'kmaq*." [58]

"In practice, the respect is expressed in the way we deal with the world around us. We will not kill an animal unless we are in danger, or require it for food, and then we give humble thanks and an offering (usually tobacco) to its spirit for giving its life for us. In exactly the same way, we will not kill a plant unless we have need of it for some purpose, and again we will make an offering in recognition of its sacrifice. In fact, we will make an offering to Mother Earth if we dig a hole, in recognition of the fact that we are disturbing her skin." [59]

"This is just so incredibly beautiful, Gabriel. Might you be able to share more?"

Gabriel smiled.

_____

[58] Mi'kmaq Spirit. *M''kmaw Culture: Spirituality* accessed on November 23, 2008 at www.muiniskw.org/pgCulture2.htm
[59] Ibid.

"Native spirituality also "demands that we recognize our place in the world around us, and never forget that we are surrounded by other beings who were created by the same supreme being that created us, and are just as deserving of life as we are." [60] Simply stated, we do not take anything we do not need, we waste nothing, and we offer thanks for everything we do take."

In essence, ma petite, one's talents "are a gift from the Creator. How you use them is the gift *you give back* to the Creator," [61] which is something that we have always taken the time to practice."

"Clearly, the westernized people of the twenty-first century have lost much to power and greed, no longer thinking about Mother Gaia. What you have shared has *always* resonated deep within my soul, for I am able to recognize the truth and the wisdom inherent in your very words."

---

[60] Mi'kmaq Spirit. *M''kmaw Culture: Spirituality* accessed on November 23, 2008 at www.muiniskw.org/pgCulture2.htm
[61] Mi'kmaq Spirit. *About the Authors* accessed on November 23, 2008 at www.muiniskw.org/pgAuthors.htm

"I now feel beckoned, Madeleine, to tell you a little bit more about Henry Sinclair, if I may."

Madeleine's eyes sparkled with excitement.

"Born in 1345, he was tall and strong. He looked like the Norse people, having blond hair and blue eyes.

"He could speak fluent Latin, Norse and Lowland Scots." [62] As well, he had also "heard all of the Norse tales of a land far west of Greenland so he persuaded two of his Venetian friends, Nicolo and Antonio Zeno, who had made vast profits from ship building to come to Orkney and join his venture." [63] It was most unfortunate that "Nicolo died after an initial exploratory voyage to Greenland, but Antonio carried on and described the events in long detailed letters to his family in Venice." [64]

---

[62] Dawe, Mark. (2008). *About Orkney Islands: Mark Dawe's Journal (Scotland)* accessed on December 11, 2008 at http://markdawe.wordpress.com/2007/12/04/about-orkney-islands/
[63] Ibid.
[64] Ibid.

"Ah, yes, Gabriel. I believe that you are speaking about the *Zeno Narratives* that were published in 1558. According to these letters, "the adventurers fitted out a small fleet and Antonio armed it with Pietro cannons which he brought from Venice." [65] It was in 1398 that "Antonio Zeno and 300 colonists set sail for the west in twelve ships. They eventually reached Newfoundland and spent their first winter in Nova Scotia," [66] if I have remembered correctly.

"It was also around this same time, that I can recollect reading about your people having a history that tells of the arrival of a prophet called Kluskap. In keeping, the Mi'kmaq "started fishing with European-style nets. A couple of hilltop ruins in Nova Scotia have been dated to this period by Canadian archaeologists and two brass cannons dredged from the Digby harbor in 1990 have been identified as

---

[65]Dawe, Mark. (2008). *About Orkney Islands: Mark Dawe's Journal (Scotland)* accessed on December 11, 2008 at
http://markdawe.wordpress.com/2007/12/04/about-orkney-islands/
[66] Ibid.

fourteenth century Pietro cannons," [67] which, surely, has to be more than mere happenstance."

"Quite right you are, ma petite. You, too, are a history lesson unto yourself, which brings me to my next point. It has been stated that Henry fathered thirteen children. Being the Scottish nobleman and explorer that he was, why, then, is it that his funerary record has never been found?"

In full recognition of the truth, all Madeleine could do was nod in contemplation. "He never did return, did he, Gabriel? Instead, he chose to remain here, living in harmony among your people."

"That is so. His title eventually passed to his grandson, William, the very same individual who commissioned and built Rosslyn Chapel."

"Perhaps this is why I have always sensed a similarity between many of the native beliefs and that of the medieval

---

[67] Dawe, Mark. (2008). *About Orkney Islands: Mark Dawe's Journal (Scotland)* accessed on December 11, 2008 at http://markdawe.wordpress.com/2007/12/04/about-orkney-islands/

Gnostic mystics, especially when each made continual reference to *the kingdom of God as residing within* each person. Clearly, Henry Sinclair also shared much of himself and his inner understanding with your people."

"I am honoured by your ability to easily discern information, transcending beyond the boundaries of the past. You must continue to allow life to proceed in accordance with your personal vision. Dearest Madeleine, you are a woman well before even your own time."

The remainder of the afternoon passed all too quickly. As evening approached, they returned to sup with Mother Pêche.

When it came time for Gabriel to depart, Madeleine felt a deep wrenching within her heart, knowing that this would be her one and only visit with him.

"Before I go, I leave you with these words of my people.

"*Msit mimajulnu'k weskwijinu'ltijik alsumsultijik aqq newte' tett wkpimte'tmut aqq koqwajo'taqnn wejkl'aqmititil* which means all human beings are born free and equal in dignity and rights. They are endowed with reason and conscience and should act towards one another in a spirit of brotherhood." [68]

It was all Madeleine could do to get past the lump that had formed in her throat.

"Rest assured, ma petite, we shall meet again after your return to the land of the twenty-first century."

With a hug and a wave, he was gone. Having gleaned much that day, Madeleine was now overcome with exhaustion, and so she slept.

---

[68] Ager, Simon. (2008). *Mikmaq Language, alphabet and pronunciation* accessed on November 23, 2008 at www.omniglot.com/writing/mikmaq.htm

Chapter 12

The morning of August 16, 1755, was a most beauteous one. Madeleine could not believe that her birthday had come full circle, once again, and yet she knew that in her own time, upon returning, she would have aged naught a single day. Taken outside of its quantum counterpart, it was still so confusing.

Madeleine also knew that it was time to begin preparing what she and Michel would have to do to get back, courtesy of the time tunnel.

In remembering what she had learned regarding the deportation of 1755, the deportation of her mother's people, time was clearly of the essence.

She knew that living successively under French, and then British rule, the Acadians were a people often forced to adapt.

The British wanted to settle permanently in the colony, so they founded the city of Halifax in 1749, their effort to reduce the influence of Louisbourg. "The new capital city would not need to be dependent on the Acadians for supplies and it could serve as the landing site for new Protestant colonists – and significant troops of soldiers. This military deployment made the Acadians nervous; some of them left for the west of Nova Scotia and others went as far as Prince Edward Island." [69]

This, of course, would mean that things were going to be changing drastically for the Acadian people, some of whom had already left their homes, trusting that they would be far better off.

In 1753, Major Charles Lawrence had been appointed governor of Nova Scotia. Not trusting the Acadians, "whom he believed were in cahoots with Natives, he threatened them with deportation to France if they refused to take the oath of allegiance to the British Crown, despite their status

---

[69] Historica. *The Deportation of the Acadians* accessed on December 7, 2008 at http://www.histori.ca/peace/page.do?pageID=275

as a politically and commercially neutral people, both in terms of the British and the French." [70]

In addition, "he petitioned the colony's court and was granted permission by the top court to carry out his threats. The decision was made easier by the fact that while most Acadians were neutral, some had already taken up arms for France. On July 28, 1755, Lawrence ordered his men to start arresting Acadians with a view to deporting them." [71]

This had already been happening. As difficult as it was to continue with the day-to-day duties while the men were being detained and arrested, all knew that striving for normalcy was the best that they could do.

Madeleine quickly pushed these thoughts away, for this was her wedding day. She was not about to let the politics of the day destroy this special beginning of her wedded life with Michel. Better yet, this occasion would give the entire village something to celebrate in a time of great uncertainty.

---

[70] Historica. *The Deportation of the Acadians* accessed on December 7, 2008 at http://www.histori.ca/peace/page.do?pageID=275
[71] Ibid.

While the actual ceremony was small, attended to only by Michel's family and a few close friends of Madeleine's, namely Mother Pêche and Gabriel Sinclair, the celebration was a grand affair back at Michel's homestead, lasting long into the evening. Madeleine looked resplendent, wearing her handwoven veil as a headdress.

Marriage played a prominent role in the lives of the Acadian people, linked to the survival of their community.

Indeed, procreation was considered the chief function of marriage. In essence, very little time went by before a young bride became pregnant, giving birth to the first of many children to come.

Madeleine knew how fortunate she was to be marrying Michel. Not only did she respect him, she loved him deeply.

What she had been able to find in Michel was what she had always been looking for. Giving a deep chuckle, she had to wonder at the synchronicity of the universe in sending her backwards in time, some 250 years, simply to find that which she had long been seeking.

Chapter 13

It was through Lawrence's order on August 11, 1755, that these words were written: "clear the whole country of bad subjects ... and disperse them among ... the colonies upon the continent of America. Collect them up by any means. Send them off to Philadelphia, New York, Connecticut and to Boston." [72]

It was on August 19, 1755, just three days following the wedding of Madeleine and Michel, that New England troops, under the command of Lieutenant Colonel John Winslow, disembarked at Grand Pré.

Marching to the center of town, Winslow quickly took possession of the parish church as his base camp. He then ordered his men to build a palisade for their defense.

---

[72] Landry, Peter. (2008). *History of Nova Scotia: Book 1, Part 6, Chapter 7: The Deportation of the Acadians: The Deportation Orders* accessed on November 16, 2008 at www.blupete.com/Hist/NovaScotiaBk1/Part6/Ch07.htm

Having had enough of the Acadians, British subjects who refused to sign the oath of allegiance, all was drawn to a dramatic halt on September 5, 1755.

Every Acadian man and boy over the age of ten was ordered to show up at the church at Saint-Charles-des-Mines.

Madeleine had begged Michel to go into hiding, so they could carry through with their plan, when the news first reached them.

He refused, saying that it was a matter of principle, that family was the pillar of the community, and that, as much as he loved her, he needed to be there to support both his father and his brothers.

Madeleine's heart was breaking, for she knew what was about to transpire. Knowing that the women and daughters of the village knew nothing about this British plan, already in motion, they continued to trust in good faith.

On the day in question, "over four hundred showed up at the appointed hour to hear the king's wishes, only to be placed under arrest. The Deportation at Grand-Pré had officially begun." [73]

Needing an interpreter, John Winslow had summoned François Landry. Landry was told that they would start the embarkation that day. It was Landry who was to read the orders that Winslow had written on that fateful day in the Saint-Charles-des-Mines church.

Gentleman, I have received from his Excellency, Governor Lawrence, the King's instructions, which I have in my hands.

---

[73] Northeast Archaeological Research. (2005). *Grand-Pré National Historic Site* accessed on November 16, 2008 at http://www.northeastarch.com/grand_pre.html

By his orders you are called together to hear His Majesty's final resolution concerning the French inhabitants of this Province of Nova Scotia, who for more than a half century have had more indulgence granted them than any of his subjects in any part of his dominions. What use you have made of it, you yourselves best know.

The duty I am now upon, though necessary, is very disagreeable to my natural make and temper, as I know it must be grievous to you, who are of the same species. But it is not my business to dwell on the orders I have received, but to obey them and, therefore, without hesitation, I shall deliver to you His Majesty's instructions and commands, which are, that your lands and tenements and cattle and livestock of all kinds be forfeited to the crown, with all your effects, except money and household goods, and that you yourselves are to be removed from this Province.

The preemptory orders of His Majesty are, that all the French inhabitants of these Districts be removed, and through his Majesty's goodness, I am directed to allow you your money and as many of your household goods as you can take without overloading the vessels you go in.

I shall do everything in my power that all these goods are secured to you and that you be not molested in carrying them away, and also that whole families shall go in the same vessel; so that this removal, which I am sensible must give you a great deal of trouble, may be made as easy as His Majesty's service will admit; and I hope that in whatever part of the world your lot may fall, you may be faithful subjects, and a peaceable and happy people.

I must also inform you, that it is in His Majesty's pleasure that you remain in the security under inspection and direction of the troops that I have the honor to command.

John Winslow [74]

---

[74] Landry, Peter. (2008). *History of Nova Scotia: Book 1, Part 6, Chapter 11: The Deportation of the Acadians: The Deportation Orders* accessed on November 16, 2008 at www.blupete.com/Hist/NovaScotiaBk1/Part6/Ch11.htm

In retrospect, the men and boys were actually housed in the church for one month before the embarkation officially began.

While it was indeed a blessing that the men had been able to complete all that was required of them for the harvesting, it may well have been part of the overall plan. Had it been otherwise, the Acadian populace might have been able to discern what was happening. Now they were being housed as political prisoners.

It was a month of excruciating uneasiness, unbeknownst to Madeleine, who also was newly pregnant.

The promise made to the Acadians, that families were not to be divided during the process, was not kept.

The motives of Charles Lawrence were not at all sympathetic to the plight of the Acadian people.

In a letter sent to Colonel Robert Monckton, Lawrence shared the following words: "I would have you not wait for the wives and the children coming in but ship off the men without them." [75]

Over the course of several days, the women and children of the village continued to gather outside the church in a line that seemed as if it went on for miles. Unsure if families were going to remain intact, there was much wailing and wringing of hands.

Many of the men had already been placed on several of the transports that lay docked in the basin.

When Madeleine finally got her first glimpse of Michel in over a month, the last male to evacuate the church, she could not believe how haggard and worn he looked, so much older than his twenty-seven years.

Mother Pêche gave her a strange and secretive look, encouraging her to advance towards him.

---

[75] Griffiths, Naomi. (1969). *The Acadian Deportation: Causes and Development* Ph.D. thesis, University of London. (p. 176).

Needing no further bolstering, she ran to him, copious tears streaming down her face.

Amidst their misery and clasped hands, a British soldier advanced towards them, placing his hand atop theirs in a genuine gesture of momentary compassion, humanity and understanding.

Looking quickly into his eyes, Madeleine realized how hard it must have been for him, also a young man, to have to follow such harsh orders.

Mere seconds later, Madeleine was overwhelmed by a sense of dizziness and nausea akin to déjà vu, fainting in a heap at the feet of the British soldier.

Coming to, she found that she had been transported back to the Grand Pré that she had left. In actual fact, she quickly assessed it to be the very same day that her time travel experience first began.

Bereft at the loss of her love, she dissolved in a heap, sobbing at the base of the statue of Evangeline.

A young man in Acadian garb approached. Bending down, he was quick to offer her a handkerchief.

After having wiped her eyes, Madeleine discovered, to her complete astonishment, that the handkerchief she now held was the very *same* one that she had lovingly weaved and embroidered for Michel.

Almost afraid to look up, she knew that she had no choice but to do so.

Their eyes met, hesitatingly at first. Sharing both a look of instant recognition and momentary disbelief, tentative smiles quickly blossomed into wide grins as they fell into each other's arms, knowing that they had made it, knowing that their love was safe.

Truly, I am not sure what propelled Michel and myself forward in time.

That very morning, Mother Pêche *insisted* that I hide my backpack, complete with the copy of the Aramaic codex that Gabriel had so lovingly presented to me, along with both the slim Latin volume and the completed translation from Latin into French, beneath my clothes.

She kept telling me that the time had come for Yeshua's book to be revealed. Perhaps, in truth, it was this relic of antiquity that allowed for our return to the time frame from whence I had come.

Having been able to settle on thirty acres of south facing, cleared farmland in Upper Granville (west of Bridgetown, situated on the majestic Annapolis River) after the birth of our daughter, Sophia, was a dream come true for both of us.

Many years have passed since this adventure. Written for me, although not in the first person style used in both my initial missive to you as well as this final message, I trust that you have enjoyed my story.

These hands, now withered and crippled with age, can no longer hold a pen to write.

Signing my name to the manuscript, prior to publication, provided the closure that was needed. I now take great satisfaction in being able to rest.

Michel and I have shared a magical life, as evidenced through our only daughter, Sophia. Interestingly enough, she was born with the very same birthmark, that of the Templar cross, but situated *between her shoulder blades*.

In the coming together of two hearts, linked in the proper manner, left breast (the feminine) against right breast (the masculine), I will leave you, the reader, to surmise what *you* feel this location of Sophia's birthmark to mean. Aside from what will probably be portrayed as pure conjecture, together, we have proven to be an extraordinary triad.

Given the nature of our genetic backgrounds, as well as current DNA research that is forever expanding to rewrite history, such is serving to depict the interconnectedness of all humankind.

In keeping with the scientific findings of the twentieth century, we know that energy cannot be destroyed.

By comparison, energy can, and often does, change its form of expression, which is *exactly* what happened to Yeshua some 2,000 years ago.

We need to be focusing on his message of resurrection, a message that simply refers to birth from an existing life, as contained within this very tome.

Whether you choose to believe or not, the ancients had a name for us, the people living out these days.

Measurements of time, some dating to 18,000 years ago, foresaw the birth of a powerful generation.

I have been proud to have lived during the *no time* as so long ago prophesied by the ancients, a time of interface between worlds.

Embrace your inner wisdom.

Embrace the knowingness that these ancient texts spoke of us when writing the words *you who walk between the worlds*, for we were the ones standing on the precipice of a brand new world.

Infinite Blessings to all who have lived these pages with me.

My name is Yeshua ben Yosef, the eldest son born to Yosef and Miryam.

During the time of my birth, in the year 3 BC, high magnetic values, for the most part, were being experienced across the planet. By comparison, Judaea was experiencing relatively low magnetic values. This was the best possible locale in which to be born, an area where people were more open and receptive to new ideas. It is for this reason that I chose to be born in this region.

These are my words.

Why am I putting them to parchment? Is it so they will be remembered for posterity? Nay, that is not my intent. Like every writer before me, I simply wish to speak my truth, so that my message cannot be misconstrued. All who read the very words contained within this codex shall be able to ascertain my alignment with truth.

I am one of you, meaning that I, too, am of the brotherhood of man.

All have come here to experience and understand the conclusiveness of God in this physical form. If you but take the time to see, to feel, to reflect, to meditate within, you will see that God exists everywhere, within all things and within all beings.

We are a melding of *God-man* (the mind of God expressing in human form) and *man-God* (physical man expressing the God within), a combined merger of spiritual and physical that serves to continue the expansion of the Father into forever.

In this light, you need not seek anything outside of your Being, for all that you need resides within.

As you come into your own alignment with truth, you, too, shall denote that anything that does not serve you, anything that is not in resonance shall fall away. You shall also be able to attest that it is in this release and letting go that something better *always* comes along.

The only constant in life is change. Be not afraid of change. Change allows all to Be (as they are) and to Become (who they truly are).

One of the most challenging tasks we face is to learn to become nonjudgmental. As you learn to let things be, disentangling from both emotionally charged situations as well as from the collective intellectual mindset of laws, rules and dogma, you are able to experience your own freedom and resolution.

Willing to embrace the higher vibration, an internal shift in consciousness takes place, thereby enabling you to Become (who you truly are).

Do not try to restrict others by judging them, controlling them or blaming them, for this limits your understanding of them. By direct association, this behavior also serves to limit their understanding of themselves.

Just as you have experienced yours, so, too, must you allow others the time and opportunity to experience their own freedom, their own resolution.

Whenever you judge people or situations, you envelop them within your own belief system. In this way, you blind yourself to the truth about them, forgetting that they, too, are whole and divine.

Many have forgotten their divinity. In so doing, they believe themselves to be separate from God. Within this forgetting lies limited beliefs, opinions and judgments, none of which are functional in navigating your way through to the higher expression of the God within.

There *is* a way to remembering the sacredness of all life, and that is the way of nonjudgment.

As you become aware of your limiting beliefs, you better understand that your interactions with others are driven by what *you believe to be true* about the person. Sadly, these limiting beliefs *never* reflect the actual truth, a truth that states all is one.

As you gain in universal awareness, you quickly come to the realization that your divinity is also theirs as well.

When you respond to people with love and compassion, you readily move from conflict to harmony. Such is the very freedom sought by all.

When you remember, embrace and share your divinity, you free others to walk their truth. You become accepting of their truth, for such is whom they are.

So, too, do you need to remember that we are *continually evolving and changing* as per our own individual experience(s). This also adds to both the greater collective experience as well as the totality of God, which means, as well, that *God is also continually evolving and changing*. How could it be otherwise for this loving energy that is ongoing and forever?

Living a life of gratitude, trust, love and peace is what generates more of the same, thereby continuously affecting those around you in a positive way.

Radiating the complete and total realization of being one with the Creator is what enables, and allows, others to feel safe and secure within your very presence.

For many of your brothers and sisters, this is *exactly* what is needed to begin to elicit an arresting change within their very Being. It is impossible *not* to experience the effects of such love and acceptance.

Long have you been taught to believe that God is perfect. I am here to offer a completely different perspective, one that many may not be ready for.

God is *not* perfect, for perfection is naught but a limitation. God simply is.

God loves us so grandly that we have been allowed, through choice and free will, to create our vast illusions of perfection and imperfection, good and evil, positive and negative.

What does this mean?

It means that God, being the totality of All That Is, is the wrong *as well as* the right, the vile ugliness *as well as* the alluring beauty, the unholiness *as well as* the divinity, the illusion *as well as* the reality.

There is no greater love than this.

We have been entrusted with the power(s) to create that which will enable us to *expand in our knowingness*. God allows us to express as we choose, without judgment.

We create the life opportunities of our choice.

We determine and select which path(s) to take. It is to be remembered that the primary tool for this journey is naught but life itself.

We alone determine how, and to what degree, we progress along our evolutionary path, moving past our illusions of limitation to the freedom that lies beyond.

Aside from love, on an immaculately grand scale, thought also holds all matter together, for *this*, too, is what God is.

It is known that thought must first exist before manifestation of thought, also known as creation, can take place. In that alignment, we have the ability to manifest whatever we wish, all for the sole purpose of enhancing the life wisdom that we continue to accrue, life after life after life.

We create our lives through our own thought processes. Everything you think, you will feel. Everything you feel, you will manifest. Everything you manifest serves to create the condition(s) of your life.

Every word we utter expresses some feeling within our souls. Every word we utter serves to create the conditions of our lives. This is a direct fusion of thought with emotion.

Many will have heard the phrase *like attracts like*, which means that what one gives thought to attracts, unto itself, the very same. In the end, it is still a matter of choice and free will.

Thought is the true giver of life that never dies, that can never be destroyed. All have used it to think themselves into life, for thought is your link to the mind of God.

We *get* what we speak. We *are* what we think. We *become* what we direct our energies to. We *become* that which we conclude ourselves to be.

That having been said, *I AM THAT I AM* is not a phrase to be taken lightly.

Hence, we are neither slave, nor servant. By comparison, we are sovereign and masterful beings. We are the creators and directors of our lives. We write the script and decide who plays the roles assigned to them.

While many continue to accept limiting thoughts, of which there are a significant number (including fear, guilt, despair, unworthiness, failure, worry, unhappiness, pity, misery, hatred, dissension, denial of self), into their lives, it must be remembered that this is neither good nor bad; coming from a place of nonjudgment, it simply is.

In the end, we must summon into mind that *everything comes down to personal choice*. Ultimately, you can create a heaven on earth for yourself just as easily as you can create your own hell. Truly the creator of our world(s), we are part of all that we see and all that has ever been.

Here is another profound truth.

While all things are derived from thought, which is God, it is equally important to realize that God is not simply one formulated thought, but the reality of *all* thoughts.

Individual truths, as held by you, as held by me, are *all* true, for each expresses the truth(s) of their experience at any given moment in time.

While there is truth in all things, so, too, is there refinement in all things. In fact, each moment serves to refine truth, which is why God is *not* a state of perfection, but rather a state of Becoming.

What all are here to inevitably learn is that you, alone, are your greatest teacher. You, alone, are your greatest friend. Cease looking outside of yourself, for the path you are to follow resides within. Only *you* can know what is needed in your soul for your own soul fulfillment. Only *you* can be the giver of your own truth.

It is a feeling, a knowingness. To *know* your truth is also to *feel* your truth. Seek what feels right within your soul. Believe in yourself.

Be willing to Become unlimited in your truth, remembering, always, that truth is ongoing, evolving, being created every moment by every thought you have.

While there is a paradox associated with truth, it is also a profound truth, no matter how contradictory it may appear.

When you have come to understand that *everything* is true and yet *nothing* is true, you shall be able to see that just as you perceive truth to be whatever you determine it to be, so may all.

In the continuation of this explanation, in the moment that you no longer give credence to a truth, it is no longer real, for you have since moved toward a new truth. When you come to understand that truth *is* and *can be* all things, then you are free, no longer enslaved to laws, rules, dogma or intellectual understanding. To learn to Become multi-faceted in your truth means that you are not *one* truth, but *all* truths.

Become who and what you truly are by *listening to the God within you*.

Become who and what you truly are by both knowing and accepting that *God speaks through feelings*, for they will be your guide to truth, directing you onward toward your individual path of enlightenment.

Compassion is who we are.

The keys to compassion lie in your ability to embrace *all* experiences as part of the one, without judgment. This is the greatest challenge that all must face as they move towards greater states of personal mastery, which is the return to your truest form.

Demonstrating love through compassionate allowing means that you must love others enough to *allow* the range of their experience. Compassion is what you *allow* yourself to Become.

It must also be remembered that, as a result of the perceived polarity of darkness and light, we have been gifted with the opportunity to view ourselves from a different perspective, all of which is both necessary and important if we are to truly know, understand and master ourselves in all ways.

Darkness, as well as light, must be embraced, complete and without judgment, for both are an essential part of creation.

If you devotedly believe in a single source of All That Is, if you legitimately believe in the conclusiveness and totality of God, then how can you possibly believe that anything of your experience(s) is other than the same source?

Live your truth, the truth that you *feel* inside. Live it. Manifest it. There is no need to seek truth. Allow yourself to Be. As long as you look outside of yourself, you will never hear the voice that resides within, the giver of all truth and the creator of All That Is.

Each individual is the true creator and controller of his life. The purpose of life is to be part of it. The key is to live life *consciously*. Likewise, we are to *live fully* and *with intent*.

As we continue to expand in both our knowingness and our wisdom, so do we continue to expand the consciousness of all life, which is what God is.

To be *happy*. To be *joyful*. To be *filled with peace*. That is the way back to the kingdom within.

To *know* that God is not separate from you. To *know* that you and God are one and the same. That is the way back to the kingdom within.

We are here to *live lives of unlimited love*. We are here to *live lives of unlimited joy*. If we choose to have these conditions in our lives, then we must first *become* that which we want to experience more fully.

We are here because we want to be here.

We are here because we want to experience the freedom and unlimitedness that God is.

We are here to live.

You are *not* your successes. You are *not* your failures. You are *not* your poverty. You are *not* your pain. You are *not* your joy. You are *not* your fear. These are merely elements of the physical experience that you are here to partake of so that you can *know yourself* in all ways.

This is what I mean when I say that while you live in this world, you are not of this world.

The path chosen by each individual is wholly unique to that person. Each path is a valid one, all leading to the same destination, all leading to their truest nature as guided by compassion. This is why I steadily say to you feel the feelings, engage the emotions, think the thoughts; for they are what shall allow you to experience yourself in all ways.

The darkness is a most powerful catalyst. This is something that must be reconciled within each and everyone.

There are many feelings and emotions that find their root in the dark, those that you have come to know as fear, rage, anger, hate, jealousy, depression, control, violation, incest, suspicion, denial, pain, judgment, illness, disease, death, greed, bitterness and retribution.

The darkness is as much a part of you as is the light. There is, however, a way to avoid the power of this darkness, a power which lies in making choices that do not embrace the dark.

Allowing darkness to exist does not mean that such has become your choice.

Allowing darkness to exist does not mean that it is condoned.

Allowing darkness to exist simply indicates that you have acknowledged the existence of this force, a force that actually serves to remind us of the exact opposite.

Every event in life serves as a catalyst that moves us into new experiences of ourselves. There is no good, no bad, no right, no wrong; it has always been our choice to expand and know ourselves in all ways.

Allowing provides you with the opportunity to transcend the polarities of light and dark, a feat that you accomplish by embracing both as equal expressions of the same force from which we come.

Compassion is your birthright. Compassion is your truest nature. Compassion allows you to view from an equal standpoint. There is no judgment.

All people express their own versions of compassion through the manner in which they conduct themselves in every waking moment.

Are you willing to forgive those who have wronged you?

Are you willing to see beyond hate towards those who oppress you?

It is only in answering yes to these questions that you can choose to Become *more than* the circumstances.

In breaking the cycles of collective response, one becomes the higher choice. Mastery of compassion means redefining what your world means to you. It is *not* about forcing change upon the world around you.

You, and only you, choose *how* you respond. As a being of compassion, you are offered the opportunity to *transcend polarity while still living within the polarity*. This is what enables you to move forward with life, a life filled with freedom, resolution and peace.

Compassion means living in trust.

Compassion means living with joy.

Living a new truth must first start with the individual.

You must have the wisdom and the courage to embrace this new life, this new truth, as your reality. This reality must then be lived in a world that may not always support that truth. This has been the undertaking of my entire earthly mission.

Life is a spiritual endeavor. You are asked to become that which you most desire in your life.

Become the peace that you seek.

Become the compassion that you desire.

Become the forgiveness that you seek.

Become the love that you desire.

Be *not afraid* to demonstrate your Becoming. The healing of this world will come about as a result of the healing of thoughts, feelings and emotions.

Who among you is willing to live the truth of a higher response?

Who among you is willing to live the truth of what life has always had to offer?

By virtue of your service to yourself and others, so, too, do you serve the Creator. In this way, you Become the greatest gift that you can offer.

Your ability to express forgiveness, allowing others the outcome of *their* own experiences, without changing the nature of who you truly are, is the highest level of mastery to which you can attain.

Therein lies the healing of all illusion, all separation, all duality.

I will say, once again, be *not afraid* to demonstrate your Becoming.

Commissioned by Nick Bunick

author of *In God's Truth*

Reprinted with permission.

Prayer of the Bodhisattva

Alone, in the presence of others, I walk through the waking dream of life.

Others see me. At the first sight of recognition, they turn away; for they have forgotten.

Together, through the waking dream of Life, we journey.

May the clarity of my vision guide your life in grace, for I am a part of you.

May my action remind you of your God within, my action is your action.

May my breath become the breath that fills your body with life.

May my soul become the food with which to nourish and quicken you.

May the words from my mouth find a place of truth within your heart.

Let my tears become water to your lips.

Allow my love to heal your body of the pain of life.

In your most healed state, may you remember your most precious gift, your divine nature.

Through our time together, may you know yourself. In that knowing, may you find your true home, your God within.

Photo by Paula Bailey

https://www.flickr.com/photos/auntiep/2262680/

Reprinted with permission.

206

Addendum

Unaware of what awaited them in the church, the Acadians were deported to several places: [1] the American colonies, [2] France, and [3] England. Many also died during the long ocean voyage.

After the Acadians boarded the ships, orders were given to burn their homes to the ground. In this way, those who had either escaped, or were planning to, would have nothing to return to.

The deportation continued until 1762. The survivors roamed, looking for a new place to call home. In 1763, after the Seven Years War and the signing of the peace treaty, some Acadians returned to Nova Scotia, only to find that they no longer owned land. It had long been redistributed to Protestant settlers.

In all, several thousand Acadians died of illness, drowning, misery and starvation, all resulting from having been most forcibly removed from their own lands.

Having first surfaced in the 16/17th century, this document appears to be a fragment from the unexpurgated Gospel of Matthew in Syriac.

The House of David

King David of Israel

(begat on the wife of Uriah the Hittite)

Solomon

Roboam

Abia

Asa

Josaphat

Joram

Ozias

A Travel in Time to Grand Pré

Joatham

Achaz

Ezechias

Manasses

Amon

Josias

Jechonias

Salathiel

Zorobabel

Abiud

Eliakim

Azor

Sadoc

Achim

A Travel in Time to Grand Pré

Eliud

Eleazar

Mathan

Jacob = Tirah

Joseph (from Arimathea) = Miriam

Jeshua

= (a) Miriam (of Bethany of the House of Saul)

A daughter (fragment missing)

= (b) Mirium (of the House of Æthiopia known as [fragment missing] Magdelene)

A son (fragment missing) (and possibly a daughter)

In accordance with this document, the following facts are rather clear.

[1] Joseph and Miriam had three sons: Jeshua, Jacob and Judah.

[2] Jeshua (Jesus) married a lady by the name of Miriam who is of the House of Bethany, of the House of Saul.

It is this very marriage that would have brought together the two kingly lines of Israel, those of the Benjamite line of Saul and that of the Davidic line. They had a daughter whose name was possibly Mary (or Miriam).

[3] There is a further liaison, or marriage, with another Mirium, of the House of Æthiopia, that we know as Mary Magdalene. They have a son and possibly a daughter by the name of Sarah. The word Æthiopia herein does not pertain to the modern country of Ethiopia. It is a Greek word that means *the land of the burnt-face people*, a term that was used for any dark-skinned person. It was also particularly used for the Arabian Semites or Nabateans (or Sabateans), whose territory surrounded the Tetrachy of Herod, with their capital at Petra.

Recent archaeological discoveries have proven that the Sabatean or Sabaean civilization lasted for some fourteen centuries, from around 800 BC to 600 AD, and included most of modern Ethiopia as well as southern Arabia.

Montgomery, Hugh. (2006). <u>The God-Kings of Europe: The Descendants of Jesus Traced Through the Odonic and Davidic Dynasties</u> (pp 28-32). San Diego, CA: The Book Tree.

Reprinted with permission.

As a completely separate aside notation, although linked somewhat, please take the time to visit *Solving the Enigma of Petra and the Nabataeans*. [76]

---

[76] Corbett, Joey. (2009). Biblical Archaeological Review. *Solving the Enigma of Petra and the Nabataeans* located at http://www.bib-arch.org/e-features/petra.asp
Accessed August 20, 2018 at
https://www.biblicalarchaeology.org/daily/ancient-cultures/ancient-near-eastern-world/solving-the-enigma-of-petra-and-the-nabataeans/

The House of Bethany

Miriam = Jeshua ben Joseph

(of the House of David the King)

A daughter Miriam = Sigismundus

A son and a daughter Ruth = Osmeus

Elchasai 1

GENERATIONS MISSING

Marthana and Martha

GENERATIONS MISSING

Maria = Ataulf

Clodomir

Mérovée the Younger

Yuri Stoyanov, a distinguished researcher based at the Warburg Institute of the University of London, is of the opinion that both Document 1 (located herein) and Document 2 were translated by the same person.

Throughout this particular genealogy, it is the female line that seems important. It is believed that this document was produced by a Cathar family who claimed descent from the Elchasai. Believed to be dated to about 428 to 430 AD, it can be surmised that it may have been produced by, or under the orders of, Clodomir.

Montgomery, Hugh. (2006). The God-Kings of Europe: The Descendants of Jesus Traced Through the Odonic and Davidic Dynasties (pp 33-35, 41). San Diego, CA: The Book Tree.

Reprinted with permission.

Madeleine's central Sinclair lineage.

[1] King Halfdan Hringsson of Sweden and Almveigu Eymundsdatter

[2] Ivar Halfdansson (Jarl of Norway) and unknown

[3] Eystein Glumra Ivarsson (Jarl) and Ascrida Rögnvaldsdatter (Countess of Oppland)

[4] Rögnvald (The Wise) Eysteinsson (1st Earl of Orkney) (Earl of Mæri) and Countess Ragnhild of Norway

[5] Hrólf the Ganger (Rollo) (1st Duke of Normandy) of Norway and Poppa of Normandy

[6] William I (Longsword) de St. Clair (2nd Duke of Normandy) and Sprota (Adela) of Senlis

[7] Richard I (The Fearless) de St. Clair (3rd Duke of Normandy) and Lady Gunner (Gunnora) de Crepon of Denmark

[8] Richard II (The Good) de St. Clair (4th Duke of Normandy) and Judith of Brittany

[9] Robert (The Magnificent) de St. Clair (6th Duke of Normandy) and Herleva (Arlette) of Falaise

[10] William I (of England) de St. Clair (7th Duke of Normandy) and Matilda (Maude) of Flanders, daughter of Count Baldwin V of Flanders and Princess Adela (Alix) Capet of France.

Winning the Battle of Hastings in 1066, William (also known as The Conqueror) was crowned King of England.

Genealogical descendancy for Matilda (Maude) of Flanders.

[1] King Halfdan Hringsson of Sweden and Almveigu Eymundsdatter

[2] Ivar Halfdansson (Jarl of Norway) and unknown

[3] Eystein Glumra Ivarsson (Jarl) and Ascrida Rögnvaldsdatter (Countess of Oppland)

[4] Rögnvald (The Wise) Eysteinsson (1st Earl of Orkney) (Earl of Mæri) and Countess Ragnhild of Norway

[5] Hrólf the Ganger (Rollo) (1st Duke of Normandy) of Norway and Poppa of Normandy

[6] Gerloc (Adele) of Normandy and Duke William III of Aquitaine

[7] Adelaide of Aquitaine and King Hugh Capet of France

[8] King Robert II of France and Constance of Arles

[9] Adela (Alix) Capet of France and Count Baldwin V of Flanders

[10] Matilda (Maude) of Flanders and William I (of England) de St. Clair (7th Duke of Normandy).

Winning the Battle of Hastings in 1066, William (also known as The Conqueror) was crowned King of England.

Genealogical descendancy for Matilda (Maude) of Flanders.

[1] Count Baldwin II of Flanders and Ælfhryth (Elfrida)

[2] Count Arnulf I (The Great) of Flanders and Adèle (Attala) of Vermandois

[3] Count Baldwin III of Flanders and Matilda of Saxony

[4] Count Arnulf II of Flanders and Rozala of Lombardy

[5] Count Baldwin IV of Flanders and Ogive of Luxembourg

[6] Count Baldwin V of Flanders and Adela (Alix) Capet of France

[7] Matilda (Maude of Flanders) and William I (of England) de St. Clair (7th Duke of Normandy).

Winning the Battle of Hastings in 1066, William (also known as The Conqueror) was crowned King of England.

Genealogical descendancy for Adela (Alix) Capet of France.

[1] Robert (The Strong) (Duke of France) Count of Orléans and Princess Adelaide

[2] King Robert I of France and Béatrice of Vermandois

[3] Hugh le Grande (The Great) and Hedwige of Saxony

[4] King Hugh Capet of France and Adelaide of Aquitaine

[5] King Robert II of France and Constance of Arles

[6] Adela (Alix) Capet of France and Count Baldwin V of Flanders

Genealogical descendancy for Ælfhryth (Elfrida).

[1] King Cerdic of the West Saxons and unknown

[2] King Cynric of the West Saxons and unknown

[3] King Ceawlin of the West Saxons and unknown

[4] Cuthwine of Wessex (did not rule) and unknown

[5] Cuthwulf (Cutha) of Wessex (did not rule) and unknown

[6] Ceolwald of Wessex (did not rule) and unknown

[7] Cenred of Wessex (did not rule) and unknown

[8] Ingild (brother of King Ine of Wessex, did not rule) and unknown

[9] Eoppa of Wessex (did not rule) and unknown

[10] Eafa of Wessex (did not rule) and unknown

[11] King Eahlmund of Kent and unknown

[12] King Egbert (of England) and Readburh

[13] King Aethelwulf (of England) and Osburh

[14] King Alfred (The Great) (of England) and Ealhswith (Alswitha) of the Gaini

[15] Ælfhryth (Elfrida) and Count Baldwin II of Flanders

KEY SOURCE

Weis, Frederick Lewis. (1988). <u>Ancestral Roots of Sixty Colonists Who Came To New England Between 1623 and 1650</u> (pp. 1-2). Baltimore, Maryland: Genealogical Publishing Company.

Genealogical descendancy for Princess Adelaide.

[1] King Pépin III of the Franks and Bertrada of Laon

[2] King Charles I (Charlemagne) and Hildegard

[3] Holy Roman Emperor Louis I (The Pious) and Ermengarde of Hesbaye

[4] Princess Adelaide and Robert (The Strong) (Duke of France) Count of Orléans

Monogram of Charlemagne from the subscription of a royal diploma: *Signum (KAROLVS) Caroli gloriosissimi regis*

Genealogical descendancy for Bertrada of Laon

[1] Bertrada of Prüm and unknown

Posited as possibly being Martin of Laon. [77]

Posited as possibly being Norbert d'Aquitaine, son of Hugobert d'Aquitaine and d'Irmine d'Oeren. [78]

[2] Count Charibert of Laon and Bertrada of Cologne

[3] Bertrada of Laon and King Pépin III of the Franks

Charlemagne ties into the Merovingian lineage through his great grandmother, Bertrada of Prüm, although there are conflicting accounts as to her parentage.

---

[77] www.stirnet.com/genie/data/ancient/fh/franks2.php#link3
[78] nobles-ancetres.pagesperso-orange.fr/Familles/Hugobert.pdf

She was either the daughter of Theuderic III of Neustria or the granddaughter of Dagobert I of Austrasia through her mother Irmina of Oeren.

In keeping with my research, I list her as the daughter of Theuderic III of Neustria.

In either case, she is his primary direct Merovingian link.

The *fictional* central LeBlanc (de Blanchefort) lineage as belongs to Michel *dit Sophie*, a line that has Merovingian connections.

[1] Theuderic de Blanchefort and Bertrada of Orléans

[2] Clovis I de Blanchefort

[3] Dagobert de Blanchefort

[4] Clotaire I de Blanchefort

[5] Childeric I de Blanchefort

[6] Clotaire II de Blanchefort

[7] Clovis II de Blanchefort

[8] Childeric II de Blanchefort

[9] Arnulf Mérovée de Blanchefort

[10] Lord Godfrey de Blanchefort of Guyenne

[11] Bertrand de Blanchefort (6th Grand Master of the Knights Templar)

[12] Michel *dit Sophie* de Blanchefort, illegitimate issue

[13] Pierre Bertrand de Blanchefort

[14] Arnulf Mérovée de Blanchefort (Templar knight who escaped from Montségur)

[15] Theuderic de Blanchefort

[16] Dagobert de Blanchefort

[17] Godfrey de Blanchefort

[18] Arnulf Mérovée de Blanchefort (accompanied Henry I Sinclair to the New World)

[19] Michel *dit Sophie* de Blanchefort (born in the New World), ancestor to Michel *dit Sophie* LeBlanc (son of Honoré LeBlanc and Geneviève Baillon)

HISTORICAL FACT

Conquered by Simon de Montfort in 1209 in what later was to become known as the Albigensian Crusade, he gave the castle, which at that time was known as Château de Blanchefort, and the surrounding lands, to his comrade in arms, Pierre de Voisons.

These lands also included Rennes-le-Château, where de Voisons made his residence in what we now know as the Château Hautpoul, a home that had belonged to the seigneurs of Rennes for centuries.

It was between 400 and 500 AD that the Visigoths settled in Rhedae (an earlier name for Rennes-le-Château). It was in 1059 that the original church at Rennes-le-Château was constructed and dedicated to Mary Magdalene.

Another aside interest of actual history is that the mother of Pope Clement was Ida de Blanchefort; she was of the same family of Bertrand de Blanchefort, 6th Grand master of the Knights Templar.

Genealogy Chart 9

The Merovingian Dynasty

[1] Clodion (Clodius V) = Princess Basina of Thuringia (daughter of Wedelphus of Thuringia)

[2] Meroveus (Mérovée) = Verica

[3] Childeric I = Queen Basina of the Thuringians

[4] Clovis I (The Great) = St. Clothilde de Burgundy

[5] Clotaire I = Aregund von Thuringia

[6] Chilperic I = Fredegund

[7] Clotaire II = Haldetrude

[8] Dagobert I = Nantilde (Nanthilda)

[9] Clovis II = Bathilde (Batilde) de France

[10] Theuderic III = Clotilde dite Doda of Herstal

[11] Bertrada of Prüm = unknown

Refer to Genealogy Chart 7.

[12] Count Caribert de Laon = Bertrada of Cologne

[13] Bertrada de Laon = Pépin III (Pépin the Short)

[14] Charlemagne (Charles I)

HISTORICAL FACT

There was evidently something very special about King Meroveus and his priestly successors, for they were accorded special veneration. They were also widely known for their esoteric knowledge and occult skills. This learned dynasty, emerging in the ancient Nazarite tradition, became known as the long-haired Sorcerer Kings. Noted sorcerers in the manner of the Samaritan Magi, they firmly believed in the hidden powers of the honeycomb. Naturally made up of hexagonal prisms, the honeycomb was considered, by philosophers, to be the manifestation of divine harmony in nature.

To the Merovingians, the bee was a most hallowed creature and, having been a sacred emblem of Egyptian royalty, it became a symbol of wisdom.

The Merovingians were not a line of created kings, but those of natural kings. Knowing their birthright, they based this natural selection and methods of ruling (by example and good works) upon King Solomon, their ancestor.

By age 20, Clovis I was a powerful leader, destined to become the most influential figure in the West. He was the first King of the Franks to unite all of the Frankish tribes under one king.

His wife, a Catholic, managed to convert him at a time when the entire Catholic Church was on the verge of collapse. Word of his conversion soon spread and everyone in his realm began converting. Had it not been to please his wife, the entire course of history in Europe would have been dramatically different, and Catholics would have been relegated to some minor sect.

Instead, the Catholic bishops now used this opportunity to manipulate the Merovingians strategically out of the picture. Clovis unwittingly fell victim to a conspiracy against the Messianic bloodline.

King Clovis died in Paris at the age of 45. His vast kingdom was divided among his four sons to rule, circa 511. This created the new political units of the Kingdoms of Reims, Orléans, Paris and Soissons.

Pépin I, or Pépin of Landen, was the Mayor of the Palace of Austrasia under the Merovingian King Dagobert I. He was also the Mayor of the Palace for Sigebert III (eldest son of Dagobert I).

Upon the death of Pépin I, in 640, Grimoald (the elder son) inherited the position. It was at this time that there was an insurrection against the child king, Sigebert III. Grimoald succeeded in saving the life of the king, thereafter becoming his close friend.

As Sigebert III was then without children, he adopted Childebert, son of Grimoald, as his own.

Upon the birth of an heir, none other than Dagobert II, Grimoald, fearing the fate of his own dynasty, kidnapped the young king and placed him in the care of the Bishop of Poitiers. He was then smuggled to Ireland. As no trace of the young king was ever found, it was easy to convince his mother that he was dead.

However, Dagobert II was educated at the Slane Monastery, near Dublin. At age 15, he married the Celtic Princess Matilde, but she died soon after and he decided to return to France, where he married a niece of the Visigoth King.

In the meantime, Grimoald had put his own son, Childebert, on the throne. After uncovering twenty years of duplicity, Dagobert II was reinstated as the rightful king in 676. He was lanced to death soon after, on December 23, 679, and the Church reinstated Childebert, the Grimoald line.

Thus began the change in the succession of royalty. It was no longer a blood right, but something that could be appointed and coronated by the Church.

Despite the popular impression, Dagobert II was not the last Merovingian king. The dynasty continued for another seventy years, until Childeric III was deposed by Pope Zachary in March 751 at the instigation of Pépin the Short. Although his parentage is uncertain (may have been either the son of Chilperic II or Theuderic IV), he is considered the last Frankish king from the Merovingian dynasty.

Once Childeric III was deposed, Pépin the Short, who was the father of emperor Charlemagne, was the first coronated king.

Thus began the line of Kings known as the Carolingians.

Bibliography

Should you wish to explore any of the topics discussed herein, feel free to add to your knowledge base either by purchasing and/or borrowing (inter-library loan is always a possibility worth exploring) any of the titles listed.

ACADIANS

Arceneaux, Leon M. (2002) <u>Beyond the Storm: An Acadian Odyssey</u>

Arsenault, Georges. (2002) <u>Acadian Legends, Folktales and Songs from Prince Edward Island</u>

Aucoin, Réjean and Tremblay, Jean-Claude. (1999) <u>The Magic Rug of Grand Pré</u>

Barrett, Wayne. (1991) <u>The Acadian Pictorial Cookbook</u>

Bleakney, J. Sherman. (2004) <u>Sods, Soil, and Spades: The Acadians at Grand Pré and Their Dykeland Legacy</u>

Boudreau, Amy. (2002) The Story of the Acadians

Boudreau, Hélène. (2008) Acadian Star

Boudreau-Vaughan, Betty. (1997) I'll Buy You An Ox: An Acadian Daughter's Bittersweet Passage Into Womanhood

Clark, Andrew Hill. (1968) Acadia: The Geography of Early Nova Scotia to 1760

Cormier-Boudreau, Marielle and Gallant, Melvin. (1991) A Taste of Acadie

Donovan, Lois. (2007) Winds of L'Acadie

Doucet, Clive. (2000) Notes from Exile: On Being Acadian

Doucet, Clive. (2004) Lost and Found in Acadie

Doucet, Clive. (2005) Acadian Homecoming

Doughty, Arthur G. (2008) The Acadian Exiles: A Chronicle of the Land of Evangeline

Faragher, John Mack. (2005) A Great and Noble Scheme: The Tragic Story of the Expulsion of the French Acadians from Their American Homeland

Gerrior, William. (2003) Acadian Awakenings: Roots and Routes, International Links, an Acadian Family in Exile

Griffiths, Naomi. (2003) The Contexts of Acadian History, 1686-1784

Griffiths, Naomi. (2004) From Migrant to Acadian: A North American Border People, 1604-1735

Hope-Simpson, Lila. (2005) Fiddles and Spoons

Jobb, Dean W. (2005) The Acadians: A People's Story of Exile and Triumph

Johnston, John and Kerr, Wayne. (2004) Grand-Pré: Heart of Acadie

Laxer, James. (2007) The Acadians: In Search of a Homeland

Longfellow, Henry Wadsworth. (1995) Evangeline: A Tale of Acadie

Mahaffie, Charles. (2003) A Land of Discord Always: Acadia from Its Beginnings to the Expulsion of Its People, 1604-1755

Maillet, Antoine. (2004) Pélagie: The Return to Acadie

Parette, Henri-Dominique. (1998) Acadians

Roberts, Charles G. D. (1898) A Sister to Evangeline: Being the Story of Yvonne de Lamourie, and How She Went Into Exile with the Villagers of Grand Pré

Roberts, Charles G. D. (2003) The Forge in the Forest: An Acadian Romance (first published in 1896)

Ross, Sally and Deveau, Alphonse. (1995) The Acadians of Nova Scotia: Past and Present

Silver, Alfred. (2002) Three Hills Home

Stewart, Sharon. (2004) <u>Dear Canada: Banished from Our Home: The Acadian Diary of Angélique Richard, Grand Pré, Acadie, 1755</u>

Tallant, Robert and Boyd Dillon, Corinne. (2001) <u>Evangeline and The Acadians</u>

CATHARISM

Arnold, John. (2001) <u>Inquisition and Power: Catharism and the Confessing Subject in Medieval Languedoc</u>

Barber, Malcolm. (2000) <u>The Cathars: Dualist Heretics in Languedoc in the High Middle Ages</u>

Burnham, Sophy. (2002) <u>The Treasure of Montségur: A Novel of the Cathars</u>

Costen, Michael. (1997) <u>The Cathars and The Albigensian Crusade</u>

Cowper, Marcus and Dennis, Peter. (2006) <u>Cathar Castles: Fortresses of the Albigensian Crusade 1209-130</u>

Craney, Glen. (2008) <u>The Fire and the Light: A Novel of the Cathars and the Lost Teachings of Christ</u>

Douzet, André. (2006) <u>The Wandering of the Grail: The Cathars, the Search for the Grail, and the Discovery of Egyptian Relics in the French Pyrenees</u>

Guirdham, Arthur. (2004) <u>The Cathars and Reincarnation</u>

Guirdham, Arthur. (2004) <u>We Are One Another</u>

Guirdham, Arthur. (2004) <u>The Lake and The Castle</u>

Hughes, Nita. (2003) <u>Past Recall: When Love and Wisdom Transcend Time</u>

Hughes, Nita. (2006) <u>The Cathar Legacy</u>

Lambert, Malcolm D. (1998) <u>The Cathars</u>

Markale, Jean. (2003) <u>Montségur and The Mystery of the Cathars</u>

Martin, Sean. (2004) <u>The Cathars: The Most Successful Heresy of the Middle Ages</u>

Mattingly, Alan. (2005) <u>Walking in the Cathar Region: Cathar Castles of South West France</u>

Moerland, Bram. (2009) <u>The Cathars</u>

O'Shea, Stephen (2001) <u>The Perfect Heresy: The Revolutionary Life and Death of the Medieval Cathars</u>

Stoyanov, Yuri. (2000) <u>The Other God: Dualist Religions from Antiquity to the Cathar Heresy</u>

Strayer, Joseph. (1992) <u>The Albigensian Crusades</u>

Vasilev, Georgi. (2007) <u>Heresy and the English Reformation: Bogomil-Cathar Influence on Wycliffe, Langland, Tyndale and Milton</u>

Weis, Rene. (2002) <u>The Yellow Cross: The Story of the Last Cathar's Rebellion Against the Inquisition, 1290-1329</u>

DNA STUDIES

Olson, Steve. (2003) <u>Mapping Human History: Genes, Race, and Our Common Origins</u>

Oppenheimer, Stephen. (2004) <u>The Real Eve: Modern Man's Journey Out of Africa</u>

Oppenheimer, Stephen. (2004) <u>Out of Eden</u>

Sykes, Bryan. (2001) <u>The Seven Daughters of Eve</u>

Sykes, Bryan. (2005) <u>Adam's Curse: The Science That Reveals Our Genetic Destiny</u>

Sykes, Bryan. (2006) <u>Saxons, Vikings and Celts: The Genetic Roots of Britain and Ireland</u>

Sykes, Bryan. (2007) <u>Blood of the Isles: Exploring the Genetic Roots of our Tribal History</u>

Wells, Spencer. (2004) <u>The Journey of Man: A Genetic Odyssey</u>

Wells, Spencer. (2007) <u>Deep Ancestry: Inside the Genographic Project</u>

HOLY BLOODLINE, HOLY GRAIL

Andrews, Richard. (1996) <u>The Tomb of God: The Body of Jesus and The Solution To A 2,000 Year Old Mystery</u>

Arimathea, Joseph of. (1999) <u>The Book of The Holy Grail</u>

Baigent, Michael; Leigh, Richard and Lincoln, Henry. (2004) <u>Holy Blood, Holy Grail</u>

Bradley, Michael. (1996) <u>Holy Grail Across the Atlantic: The Secret History of Canadian Discovery and Exploration</u>

Bradley, Michael. (1998) <u>Grail Knights of North America: On the Trail of the Grail Legacy in Canada and the United States</u>

Bradley, Michael. (2005) <u>Swords at Sunset: Last Stand of North America's Grail Knights</u>

Emerys, Chevalier. (2007) <u>Revelation of the Holy Grail</u>

Francke, Sylvia. (2007) <u>The Tree of Life and The Holy Grail: Ancient and Modern Spiritual Paths and the Mystery of Rennes-le-Château</u>

Gardiner, Philip and Osborn, Gary. (2006) <u>The Serpent Grail: The Truth Behind the Holy Grail, the Philosopher's Stone and the Elixir of Life</u>

Gardner, Laurence. (2000) Genesis of the Grail Kings: The Explosive Story of Genetic Cloning of and the Ancient Bloodline of Jesus

Gardner, Laurence. (2001) Bloodline of the Holy Grail: The Hidden Lineage of Jesus Revealed

Gardner, Laurence. (2006) The Magdalene Legacy: The Jesus and Mary Bloodline Conspiracy

Gardner, Laurence. (2008) The Grail Enigma: The Hidden Heirs of Jesus and Mary Magdalene

Johnson, Bettye. (2005) Secrets of the Magdalene Scrolls: The Forbidden Truth of the Life and Times of Mary Magdalene

Johnson, Bettye. (2007) Mary Magdalene, Her Story

Lincoln, Henry. (2004) The Holy Place: Sauniere and the Decoding of the Mystery of Rennes-le-Château

Miles, Rosalind. (2002) The Child of the Holy Grail

Ortenberg, Veronica. (2006) In Search of The Holy Grail

Phillips, Graham. (2001) The Marian Conspiracy: The Hidden Truth About the Holy Grail, The Real Father of Christ

Pinkham, Mark Amaru. (2004) Guardians of the Holy Grail: The Knights Templar, John the Baptist, and the Water of Life

Simmans, Graham. (2007) Jesus After The Crucifixion: From Jerusalem to Rennes-le-Château

Twyman, Tracy R. (2004) The Merovingian Mythos and the Mystery of Rennes-le-Château

Wallace-Murphy, Tim and Hopkins, Marilyn. (2000) Rosslyn: Guardian of the Secret of the Holy Grail

Wallace-Murphy, Tim; Simmons, Graham and Hopkins, Marilyn. (2000) Rex Deus: The True Mystery of Rennes-le-Château

Young, John K. (2003) Sacred Sites of the Knights Templar: Ancient Astronomers and Freemasons at Stonehenge, Rennes-le-Château and Santiago de Compostela

KNIGHTS TEMPLAR

Addison, Charles G. (1997) <u>History of the Knights Templar</u>

Barber, Malcolm. (1993) <u>The Trial of the Templars</u>

Bradley, Michael. (1996) <u>Holy Grail Across the Atlantic: The Secret History of Canadian Discovery and Exploration</u>

Bradley, Michael. (1998) <u>Grail Knights of North America: On the Trail of the Grail Legacy in Canada and the United States</u>

Bradley, Michael. (2005) <u>Swords at Sunset: Last Stand of North America's Grail Knights</u>

Bradley, Michael. (2008) <u>The Secrets about the Freemasons</u>

Gardner, Laurence. (2007) <u>The Shadow of Solomon: The Lost Secret of the Freemasons Revealed</u>

Knight, Christopher and Lomas, Robert. (2001) <u>The Hiram Key: Pharaohs, Freemasonry, and the Discovery of the Secret Scrolls of Jesus</u>

Knight, Christopher and Lomas, Robert. (2001) <u>Second Messiah: Templars, the Turin Shroud and the Great Secret of Freemasonry</u>

Mann, William. (2004) <u>The Knights Templar in the New World: How Henry Sinclair Brought the Grail to Acadia</u>

Mann, William. (2006) <u>The Templar Meridians: The Secret Mapping of the New World</u>

Picknett, Lynn and Prince, Clive. (1998) <u>The Templar Revelation: Secret Guardians of the True Identity of Christ</u>

Picknett, Lynn and Prince, Clive. (2007) <u>The Turin Shroud: How Da Vinci Fooled History</u>

Pinkham, Mark Amaru. (2004) <u>Guardians of the Holy Grail: The Knights Templar, John the Baptist, and the Water of Life</u>

Read, Paul Piers. (1999) <u>The Templars</u>

Robinson, John J. (1991) <u>Dungeon, Fire and Sword</u>

Sora, Steven. (1999) The Lost Treasure of the Knights Templar: Solving the Oak Island Mystery

Sora, Steven. (2004) Lost Colony of the Templars

Wallace-Murphy, Tim and Hopkins, Marilyn. (2007) Templars in America

Wallace-Murphy, Tim. (2008) The Knights of the Holy Grail: The Secret History of the Knights Templar

Young, John K. (2003) Sacred Sites of the Knights Templar: Ancient Astronomers and Freemasons at Stonehenge, Rennes-le-Château and Santiago de Compostela

MEROVINGIANS

Baird, Robert Bruce. (2008) Merovingians: Past and Present Masters

Gardner, Laurence. (2003) Realm of the Ring Lords: The Myth and Magic of the Grail Quest

Geary, Patrick J. (1994) Before France and Germany: The Creation and Transformation of the Merovingian World

Murray, Alexander Callander. (2000) <u>From Roman to Merovingian Gaul: A Reader</u>

Murray, Alexander Callander. (2005) <u>Gregory of Tours: The Merovingians</u>

Wallace-Hadrill, J. M. (1982) <u>The Long-Haired Kings and Other Studies in Frankish History</u>

Wood, I. (1995) <u>The Merovingian Kingdoms, 450-751</u>

METAPHYSICS AND SPIRITUALITY

Ambrose, Kala. (2007) <u>9 Life Altering Lessons: Secrets of the Mystery Schools Unveiled</u>

Braden, Gregg. (1995) <u>Awakening to Zero Point: The Collective Initiation</u>

Braden, Gregg. (1997) <u>Walking Between the Worlds: The Science of Compassion</u>

Braden, Gregg. (2000) <u>The Isaiah Effect: Decoding the Lost Science of Prayer and Prophecy</u>

Braden, Gregg. (2000) Beyond Zero Point: The Journey to Compassion

Braden, Gregg, (2004) The God Code: The Secret of Our Past, The Promise of Our Future

Braden, Gregg. (2004) The Divine Name: Sounds of the God Code (audio book)

Braden, Gregg. (2005) The Lost Mode of Prayer (audio CD)

Braden, Gregg. (2005) Unleashing The Power of The God Code: The Mystery and Meaning of the Message in Our Cells (audio CD)

Braden, Gregg. (2005) An Ancient Magical Prayer: Insights from the Dead Sea Scrolls (audio book)

Braden, Gregg. (2005) Speaking the Lost Language of God: Awakening the Forgotten Wisdom of Prayer, Prophecy and the Dead Sea Scrolls (audio book)

Braden, Gregg. (2005) Awakening the Power of A Modern God: Unlock the Mystery and Healing of Your Spiritual DNA (audio book)

Braden, Gregg. (2006) Secrets of The Lost Mode of Prayer

Braden, Gregg. (2007) The Divine Matrix: Bridging Time, Space, Miracles and Belief

Bunick, Nick. (1998) In God's Truth

Chopra, Deepak. (1998) The Path to Love: Spiritual Strategies for Healing

Chopra, Deepak. (2005) Peace Is The Way: Bringing War and Violence to An End

Coelho, Paulo. (1998) The Alchemist

Coelho, Paulo. (2003) Warrior Of The Light

Das, Lama Surys. (1998) Awakening the Buddha Within

Das, Lama Surys. (2000) Awakening to the Sacred: Creating a Spiritual Life From Scratch

Das, Lama Surys. (2001) Awakening the Buddhist Heart: Integrating Love, Meaning and Connection Into Every Part of Your Life

Das, Lama Surys. (2003) <u>Living Kindness: The Buddha's Ten Guiding Principles for a Blessed Life</u>

Das, Lama Surys. (2003) <u>Letting Go of the Person You Used To Be: Lessons on Change, Loss and Spiritual Transformation</u>

Doucette, Michele. (2007) <u>The Ultimate Enlightenment For 2012: All We Need Is Ourselves</u> (ebook)

Doucette, Michele. (2008) <u>Turn Off The TV and Turn On Your Mind</u> (ebook)

Dyer, Wayne. (1998) <u>Manifest Your Destiny: The Nine Spiritual Principles For Getting Everything That You Want</u>

Dyer, Wayne. (2002) <u>Getting in the Gap: Making Conscious Contact with God Through Meditation</u> (book and CD)

Gawain, Shakti. (1993) <u>Living In The Light: A Guide to Personal and Planetary Transformation</u>

Gawain, Shakti. (1999) *The Four Levels of Healing*

Gawain, Shakti. (2000) <u>The Path of Transformation: How Healing Ourselves Can Change The World</u>

Gawain, Shakti. (2003) <u>Reflections in The Light: Daily Thoughts and Affirmations</u>

Hansard, Christopher. (2003) <u>The Tibetan Art of Positive Thinking</u>

Hicks, Esther and Hicks, Jerry. (2004) <u>Ask and It Is Given: Learning to Manifest Your Desires</u>

Hicks, Esther and Hicks, Jerry. (2005) <u>The Amazing Power of Deliberate Intent: Living the Art of Allowing</u>

Hicks, Esther and Hicks, Jerry. (2006) <u>The Law of Attraction: The Basics of the Teachings of Abraham</u>

Hicks, Esther and Hicks, Jerry. (2008) <u>The Astonishing Power of Emotions: Let Your Feelings Be Your Guide</u>

Hicks, Esther and Hicks, Jerry. (2009) <u>The Vortex: Where The Law of Attraction Assembles all Cooperative Relationships</u>

Katz, Jerry. (2007) <u>One: Essential Writings on Nonduality</u>

Koven, Jean-Claude. (2004) <u>Going Deeper: How To Make Sense of Your Life When Your Life Makes No Sense</u>

Lama, Dalai. (2004) <u>The Wisdom of Forgiveness: Intimate Conversations and Journey</u>

McTaggart, Lynne. (2003) <u>The Field: The Quest For The Secret Force Of The Universe</u>

McTaggart, Lynne. (2008) <u>The Intention Experiment: Using Your Thoughts to Change Your Life and the World</u>

Millman, Dan. (1990) <u>Way of the Peaceful Warrior</u>

Millman, Dan. (1991) <u>Sacred Journey of the Peaceful Warrior</u>

Millman, Dan. (1992) <u>No Ordinary Moments: A Peaceful Warrior's Guide to Daily Life</u>

Millman, Dan. (1995) <u>The Life You Were Born To Live</u>

Millman, Dan. (1999) <u>Everyday Enlightenment</u>

Nichols, L. Joseph (2000) <u>The Soul As Healer: Lessons in Affirmation, Visualization and Inner Power</u>

Peniel, Jon. (1998) <u>The Lost Teachings of Atlantis: The Children of The Law of One</u>

Peniel, Jon. (1999) <u>The Golden Rule Workbook: A Manual for the New Millennium</u>

Price, John Randolph. (1987) <u>The Superbeings</u>

Price, John Randolph. (1998) <u>The Success Book</u>

Quinn, Gary. (2003) <u>Experience Your Greatness: Give Yourself Permission To Live</u> (audio CD)

Redfield, James. (1995) <u>The Celestine Prophecy</u>

Redfield, James. (1997) <u>The Celestine Vision: Living the New Spiritual Awareness</u>

Redfield, James. (1998) <u>The Tenth Insight</u>

Redfield, James. (1999) <u>The Secret of Shambhala</u>

Renard, Gary. (2004) <u>The Disappearance of the Universe</u>

Renard, Gary. (2006) <u>Your Immortal Reality: How To Break the Cycle of Birth and Death</u>

Ruiz, Don Miguel. (1997) <u>The Four Agreements: A Practical Guide to Personal Freedom</u>

Ruiz, Don Miguel. (1999) <u>The Mastery of Love: A Practical Guide to The Art of Relationship</u>

Ruiz, Don Miguel. (2000) <u>The Four Agreements Companion Book</u>

Ruiz, Don Miguel. (2004) <u>The Voice of Knowledge: A Practical Guide to Inner Peace</u>

Ruiz, Don Miguel. (2009) <u>Fifth Agreement: A Practical Guide to Self-Mastery</u>

Schuman, Helen. (1997) <u>A Course in Miracles</u>

Schwartz, Robert. (2009) <u>Your Soul's Plan: Discovering the Real Meaning of the Life You Planned Before You Were Born</u>

Sharma, Robin. (1997) <u>The Monk Who Sold His Ferrari</u>

Sharma, Robin. (2005) <u>Big Ideas to Live Your Best Life: Discover Your Destiny</u>

Shinn, Florence Scovel. (1989) <u>The Wisdom of Florence Scovel Shinn</u>

Shinn, Florence Scovel. (1991) <u>The Game of Life Affirmation and Inspiration Cards: Positive Words For A Positive Life</u>

Shinn, Florence Scovel. (2006) <u>The Game of Life</u> (book and CD)

Tolle, Eckhart. (1999) <u>The Power of Now: A Guide to Spiritual Enlightenment</u>

Tolle, Eckhart. (2001) <u>Practicing the Power of Now: Meditations, Exercises and Core Teachings for Living the Liberated Life</u>

Tolle, Eckhart. (2001) <u>The Realization of Being: A Guide to Experiencing Your True Identity</u> (audio CD)

Tolle, Eckhart. (2003) <u>Stillness Speaks</u>

Tolle, Eckhart. (2003) <u>Entering The Now</u> (audio CD)

Tolle, Eckhart. (2005) <u>A New Earth: Awakening to Your Life's Purpose</u>

Twyman, James. (1998) <u>Emissary of Peace: A Vision of Light</u>

Twyman, James. (2000) <u>The Secret of the Beloved Disciple</u>

Twyman, James. (2000) <u>Portrait of the Master</u>

Twyman, James. (2000) <u>Praying Peace: In Conversation with Gregg Braden and Doreen Virtue</u>

Twyman, James. (2008) <u>The Moses Code: The Most Powerful Manifestation Tool in the History of the World</u>

Twyman, James. (2009) <u>The Kabbalah Code: A True Adventure</u>

Twyman, James. (2009) <u>The Proof: A 40-Day Program for Embodying Oneness</u>

Vanzant, Iyanla. (2000) <u>Until Today</u>

Virtue, Doreen. (1997) The Lightworker's Way

Virtue, Doreen. (2006) Divine Magic: The Seven Sacred Secrets of Manifestation (book and CD)

Walker, Ethan III. (2003) The Mystic Christ: The Light of Non-Duality and the Path of Love According to the Life and Teachings of Jesus

Walsch, Neale Donald. (1999) Abundance and Right Livelihood: Applications for Living

Walsch, Neale Donald. (2000) Bringers of The Light

Walsch, Neale Donald. (2002) The New Revelations: A Conversation with God

Walters, J. Donald. (2000) Awaken to Superconsciousness: How To Use Meditation for Inner Peace, Intuitive Guidance and Greater Awareness

Walters, J. Donald. (2000) Meditations to Awaken Superconsciousness: Guided Meditations on The Light (audio cassette)

Walters, J. Donald. (2003) <u>Meditation for Starters</u> (book and CD)

Walters, J. Donald. (2003) <u>Metaphysical Meditations</u> (audio CD)

Walters, J. Donald. (2003) <u>Secrets of Bringing Peace On Earth</u>

Weiss, Brian. (2001) <u>Messages From the Masters: Tapping Into The Power of Love</u>

Weiss, Brian. (2002) <u>Meditation: Achieving Inner Peace and Tranquility in Your Life</u> (book and CD)

Williamson, Marianne. (1996) <u>A Return To Love</u>

Williamson, Marianne. (1997) <u>Morning and Evening Meditations and Prayers</u>

Williamson, Marianne. (2002) <u>Everyday Grace: Having Hope, Finding Forgiveness and Making Miracles</u>

Williamson, Marianne. (2003) <u>Being In Light</u> (audio CD set)

Yogananda, Paramahansa. (1979) <u>Metaphysical Meditations: Universal Prayers, Affirmations and Visualizations</u>

Yogananda, Paramahansa. (2004) <u>The Second Coming of Christ: The Resurrection of the Christ Within You</u>

Zukav, Gary. (1998) <u>The Seat of The Soul</u>

Zukav, Gary. (2001) <u>Thoughts from The Seat of The Soul: Meditations for Souls in Process</u>

Zukav, Gary and Francis, Linda. (2001) <u>The Heart of The Soul: Emotional Awareness</u>

Zukav, Gary and Francis, Linda. (2003) <u>The Mind of The Soul: Responsible Choice</u>

Zukav, Gary and Francis, Linda. (2003) <u>Self-Empowerment Journal: A Companion to The Mind of The Soul: Responsible Choice</u>

Zukav, Gary. (2010) <u>Spiritual Partnership: The Journey to Authentic Power</u>

SPIRITUAL THRILLERS

Asensi, Matilde. (2006) The Last Cato

Berry, Steve. (2006) The Templar Legacy

Brown, Dan. (2003) The Da Vinci Code

Brown, Dan. (2009) The Lost Symbol

Caldwell, Ian and Thomason, Dustin. (2004) The Rule of Four

Christopher, Paul. (2006) The Lucifer Gospel

Christopher, Paul. (2009) The Sword of the Templars

Doetsch, Richard. (2006) The Thieves of Heaven

Hougan, Jim. (2006) The Magdalene Cipher

Khoury, Raymond. (2005) The Last Templar

Khoury, Raymond. (2007) The Sanctuary

Malarkey, Tucker. (2006) Resurrection

Mosse, Kate. (2007) <u>Labyrinth</u>

Navarro, Julia. (2004) <u>The Brotherhood of the Holy Shroud</u>

Navarro, Julia. (2008) <u>The Bible of Clay</u>

Ray, Tim. (2003) <u>Starbrow: A Spiritual Adventure</u>

Ray, Tim. (2004) <u>Starwarrior: Starbrow's Spiritual Adventure Continues</u>

Sierra, Javier. (2004) <u>The Secret Supper</u>

Sierra, Javier. (2007) <u>The Lady in Blue</u>

Young, Robyn. (2007) <u>Brethren: An Epic Adventure of the Knight's Templar</u>

Young, Robyn. (2008) <u>Crusade</u>

Young, Robyn. (2009) <u>The Fall of the Templars</u>

An avid reader and researcher, Michele Doucette has always been fascinated with history. Equally as passionate about genealogy, she has spent the last fifteen years validating, sourcing and accruing pertinent documents related to her own family histories.

A successful mtDNA recipient (of the U6a haplogroup, attributed to her most distant maternal Acadian ancestor, Edmée Lejeune), she continues to encourage others to do the same, *especially* in light of the fact that current DNA testing is clearly serving to both prove and rewrite history.

She credits Nick Bunick, subject of <u>The Messengers: A True Story of Angelic Presence and the Return to the Age of Miracles</u>, for leading her into the adventurous realms of the metaphysical unknown.

As a result, she has been managing the website, Portals of Spirit, since the dawn of the millennium.

She holds firm in her belief that the quality of our world depends upon the quality of our thoughts as individuals.

While she has written several e-books of a spiritual nature, <u>The Ultimate Enlightenment For 2012: All We Need Is Ourselves</u> and <u>Turn Off The TV and Turn On Your Mind</u>, this author shows that she has what it takes to make a most successful transition from research writer to novelist.

As is most often the case with writers, she is currently researching for the sequel, <u>Back Home With Evangeline</u>.

A native of Truro, Nova Scotia (referred to as Cobequid during the time of the Acadian people), she has been living on the west coast of Newfoundland since 1985.

Employed as a Special Education teacher, she feels blessed to work with such *Mighty Spirits*.

www.ingramcontent.com/pod-product-compliance
Lightning Source LLC
Chambersburg PA
CBHW060535260626
47161CB00003B/906